I0772921

Hidden in the Book
Book 1: Map of the Lost

Alan Van Ormer

ISBN-13: 978-1-962168-81-6

Chapter 1

Chase Connor had to lean over to hear the whispering voice of Alanna Nugent, the wife of a multi-million-dollar construction company owner, who was suing her ex-husband for ten million dollars. She felt it was only right since she caught him in bed with another gal on the night of their tenth anniversary, which Chase could never understand because Mrs. Nugent was beautiful with her black hair, hazel eyes, and fine figure.

"Chase, what is taking so long to make a decision?"

Chase adjusted his black tie pressed against his white shirt. "The judge has to make sure he has all the facts in place before he renders a verdict."

She touched his hand, which he quickly pulled away. "Do you believe he'll rule in his favor?"

"I can't imagine that happening, but in court you can't rule out anything. Just keep your fingers crossed."

Alanna was prepared to say something else when the judge walked out into the courtroom. "All rise," the bailiff said.

Once everyone was seated, the judge peered over at Alanna and then at her husband, who sat at another table with his attorney. "Mr. Nugent, I find it really hard to imagine why you would sleep with another woman on your anniversary night, especially after ten years of marriage. What were you thinking? Never mind, don't answer that."

The judge turned back to Alanna. "I'm sorry about what happened between you and your husband, but I find it hard to grant your request for ten million dollars."

Chase noticed her husband's sigh of relief as well as Alanna's frustrated expression.

"However," the judge continued. "Your wife should not leave this courtroom with nothing, so it is my decision that you pay your wife two million dollars. Hopefully, the two of you can move on with your lives." The judge smacked his gavel, rose, and left the courtroom.

Alanna turned to Chase with a smile.

"What are you smiling about? You wanted ten million dollars and received only two million."

"My dear boy, I never wanted ten million dollars, I just wanted enough money to start my own business."

Chase rolled his eyes. "And what kind of business might that be?"

"I'm going to buy myself a fishing boat and go on fishing cruises in the Pacific Ocean. I've always loved the water. Thank you for your help," she said, reaching out her hand to shake his.

They both turned to her ex-husband who walked over. "Are you satisfied? All you had to do was ask me for the money, and I would have helped you get started."

Alanna grinned. "It was much more exciting taking a womanizer to court and getting the money that way."

Chase stood there scratching his head as the two walked out of the courtroom holding hands.

"You should know better than trying to figure out the rich—you being one yourself."

Chase turned to the voice. "Oh my gosh, Dr. Boyd, what are you doing here? I thought you were in Montana or Idaho or somewhere where it's cold."

"That's where I am, but I had to pay one last visit to the warm confines of California before I settled down. I see you had another win."

Chase eyed him. "She asked for ten million dollars."

Dr. Boyd shook his head. "The judge was never going to give her that, and she knew it, so she's happy with what she got. I'm surprised those two weren't divorced several years ago, since he's always been into other women."

"That's what I found out in my research for this case, but sleeping with another woman on their anniversary night has to top it all."

Dr. Boyd laughed. "My boy, even though you have money, you have a lot to learn about the rich."

"Apparently, so what brings you to Los Angeles and to this courtroom today?"

"I have a proposal for you if you're interested?"

Chase clapped the older man's shoulder. "Let me wrap up some items from this case, and I'll meet you downtown at our favorite bar."

"I'll be waiting."

Chase hurried back to the office to finish his notes.

After each case, he jotted down any information that might be useful, if perchance he needed it in the future. The partners appreciated his commitment to his craft. He'd just turned twenty-six, having spent the last three years working at his father's law firm after graduating from Stanford. The partners had high hopes for him, but after his first full year, Chase wasn't too keen about continuing to be an attorney.

He turned to a soft voice and peered up at Evie Kingston standing in the doorway. She moseyed in and leaned a hip on the side of his desk. She had beautiful blue eyes, lengthy red hair, and a voice that sounded like fine brandy. "How about joining me for a nightcap at my apartment."

Chase smiled. "Not tonight, Evie, I have another commitment."

Her lower lip protruded. "Three straight times you've turned me down."

"I'm just not feeling it tonight. Sorry."

Her eyes narrowed. "You sure seemed to be feeling it the last few times at my apartment. Is there someone else?"

He shook his head. "It's a long story, and I'm really not in the mood to tell you about it."

She stood up and pushed his papers toward him. "Fine, don't expect to come crawling back to me when you're done being a mama's boy."

"What are you talking about?" He leaned over and grabbed her arm. She pulled her arm away. "Everyone knows that your family pulls all your strings. They got you this job, and your mother has you wrapped around her finger. When was the last time you dated a gal who your mother didn't approve of?" Before he could even answer, Evie answered for him. "Never. If she hadn't approved of me, we would have never been together. Everyone in the business realizes that but you."

Chase blew out a deep breath. "Wow, I'm glad I found out that you become a bit snippy when things don't go your way before we went any further. You realize the partners aren't too keen on office romance."

Her eyes lit up. "You thought there could be more between the two of us?"

"I had hoped so but not now, and it has nothing to do with what just happened."

She put her hands on her hips. "Then what is it?"

He stood up. "I really have to go now." Chase dashed out of the office, caught an elevator, and made his way down to his car in the employee parking lot. As he drove toward the bar and grill, Chase thought about Dr. Boyd. The guy was in his late fifties, a former professor at Stanford University, where Chase had earned his law degree. Dr. Boyd had always been his favorite professor because of the way he used the Socratic method, making sure the students earned their grade rather than memorizing notes from lectures.

He had last heard that Dr. Boyd was set to retire, moving to a small town in Montana to take over a law firm that handled everything from divorces to injury law. After twenty years of teaching, he was ready to get back into the grind of lawyering.

Thirty minutes later, Chase pulled into the restaurant where they had planned to meet. He hurried in and saw Dr. Boyd sitting at a corner table sipping on what looked like a strawberry daiquiri. Another drink, a rum and coke, sat at the seat in front of him. Dr. Boyd knew it had been Chase's favorite drink. Chase slipped into the seat.

"Rum and coke, like you ordered," Dr. Boyd said. They both laughed. Dr. Boyd gazed at Chase. "I was proud to see one of my prize pupils in court today. You've grown a lot in twelve months, but I didn't expect anything different."

They both turned to the server who brought over a platter of appetizers that included mozzarella stickers, chicken wings, and a couple of different dips. Chase grabbed a chicken wing. "Thank you, I'm so hungry."

Dr. Boyd laughed. "More is coming since it's all-you-can-eat-appetizers night. A perfect choice because I'm hungry also." He finished off a mozzarella stick. "How is your family and Connor and Associates faring?"

"They're as busy as ever, and I don't know how they keep it up. It's draining at times. Micah's wife just had her second child a month ago, Arthur is divorced, and Samantha finally married the guy she has two kids with. My oldest brother, Keenan, continues to sit in a rocking chair in the living room doing who knows what."

Dr. Boyd sipped his daiquiri. "And what about you?"

Chase laughed. "I was just told I'm a momma's boy."

Dr. Boyd joined him in laughter. "Wow, you're far from a momma's boy; in fact, I'm surprised you even listen to either of your parents."

"It's hard at times, but they do give some good advice, especially on how not to choose a gal for me. What brings you back to California? I thought you were on your way to Montana or somewhere near there."

After Dr. Boyd moved his drink to the side, he peered at Chase. "Are you happy here?"

Chase thought for a moment. "I love the weather, but no, I'm not happy with the current situation. Too many eighty-hour weeks, bosses who skim the law, and I'm assigned cases no one else wants since they're sure they can't win."

Dr. Boyd grinned. "How many have you lost?"

"One or two, if you count today. What are you up to?"

He searched the room and turned back to Chase. "As you know I'm taking over a law firm in Mountain Ridge, Montana, and I want you to join me. Before you say no, let me explain a couple of things. First, you'd be working on criminal cases, civil lawsuits, family law, you name it. Second, everything is so much more laid back in Montana. There's no traffic to fight, you can stare out your window and see the Rocky Mountains instead of a skyscraper, and you're able to build relationships with your clients."

Chase stirred his drink. "It sounds wonderful, but to be truthful, I'm not too sure I want to continue in the field. After a year, I'm fairly certain law's not for me. I need something different, more satisfying. I just know it's not being an attorney."

Dr. Boyd sighed. "That's damn disappointing, but you're interested in a career change? You love books, and your collection of old and rare books is top-notch. There's a small bookstore in Mountain Ridge that needs an owner. You'd be interested in something like that."

His eyes lit up. "Now that is something I will think about."

Chapter 2

The mirror in the makeup room was a little off, so Sophia Shepherd adjusted the lighting before she started putting on her makeup for her upcoming walk down the runway. Since she'd turned seventeen, Sophia had walked many a runway around the world. Now twenty-five she was preparing for the final show in Paris. She wasn't sure if she wanted to continue modeling, but her parents told her it was a wonderful occupation since she brought in at least six figures a year. Her treasure chest held more than seven million dollars.

Sophia always worked the four main fashion shows—Paris, New York City, Milan, Italy, and London each year. When not overseas, she modeled for shows throughout the U.S. She remembered back when at seventeen a designer had approached her about modeling clothes for a fashion show in Helena. After graduation she hit the circuit, and this was her seventh season in Paris.

Sophia sprayed some light tint on her strawberry-blond hair to make it shimmer a bit more, as she did with her eyelids around her emerald-green eyes. Then she added contours to her face, before finishing with a light green polish on her fingernails. She double-checked herself in the mirror.

A rough voice came from behind her, and a man put his hands on her shoulders. "Beautiful as always. Are you ready?"

She turned around and smiled up at Franklin Arthur, who had been her manager since she was seventeen. "I believe I am."

"Stand up and let me take a look at you."

She rose to her full height, and with her high heels, she was two inches taller than Franklin's five-nine height, the same height as hers without heels. At first it bothered her being as tall as her manager, but after a while she became used to it. She twirled around for him.

"Gorgeous. You'll knock them out again. Afterward, we have a dinner date with some major designers at the Marriott Paris Opera Ambassador Hotel. They're interested in your help in designing a new line of clothes."

Sophia didn't say anything.

He continued. "Then after dinner, I have other plans for the two of us."

This time she took a deep breath.

"Is everything okay?"

She brushed her hair out of her eyes. "It's been a long week, and I'm so tired. Would it be okay if I took a raincheck? I thought maybe I could just head back to the hotel to get some rest before flying to Montana tomorrow."

He grinned. "Speaking of flying to Montana, I have

some wonderful news for you, I've decided to join you. I haven't met your parents, and if we're going to continue with our relationship, it's about time I did. Isn't that wonderful?"

She pasted a polite smile on her face. "Wonderful."

Over the next hour, Sophia, along with other models, displayed unique designs—exaggerated fashion accessories like XL zippers, buckles, and buttons. Then she modeled more classic styles like tweed blazers, miniskirts, and gowns.

Sophia finished at eight-thirty, stifling a yawn. When she entered her dressing room, Franklin was waiting for her. He kissed her on the cheek.

"Marvelous. I especially enjoyed the look of the mini skirt."

She waved a dismissive hand. "You've always liked my legs."

"Among other things," he said, squeezing her arms.

She gasped. "Ouch, that hurts. Don't be so rough."

"I'm sorry. Why don't you get changed, and we'll head to the hotel. Please dress in something appropriate for the evening."

Once Franklin left, Sophia slipped off her dress. At times his overbearing ways made her sick. He was her manager, but he'd also turned into her lover, something she regretted more each day. When they first started together, she was infatuated with him because he was sixteen years older than her, and at seventeen, that was a big difference. Now that he was forty-one, it wasn't as fascinating.

Sophia slipped into a long green dress with two-inch heels, reached into her pocketbook, and grabbed a small porcelain box. Checking to make sure no one was around, then shoved two diet pills into her mouth. She detested taking the pills, but they were the only ones keeping her at a comfortable weight, although she knew the pills had adverse effects on her organs. The practice had started six months ago, and she knew she must get off them soon or else suffer the risks.

Twenty minutes later she met Franklin at the doorway. He frowned. "What took you so long?"

She offered a pert smile. "I had to pretty myself up for this meeting."

His frown turned into a grin. "And you do look appetizing."

Sophia sighed. "When you talk like that, it sounds so vulgar, as if I'm some kind of piece of meat that you want to devour."

He didn't say anything, but Sophia had the feeling that's exactly how he felt about her. The two arrived at the hotel thirty minutes later. Once they climbed out of the cab, Sophia looked up at the hotel's facade of white stones. She recognized the traditional style of Baron Haussmann.

For a quick moment, Sophia thought back about a book she had read about Paris architecture. She loved books. Georges-Eugene Haussmann, commonly known as Baron Haussmann, was chosen by Emperor Napoleon III to do an urban renewal plan of new boulevards, parks, and public works in Paris.

"Let's go, Sophia. Quit dawdling."

He stuck out his elbow, she placed her hand through it, and they walked into the lobby. Her eyes took in the whole place. The art deco features of the elegant glass ceilings took her breath away. They headed to a back room where several people were chatting.

A short man who had light hair and a curly mustache joined them. "Franklin Arthur, I'm glad you could join us, and this must be your lovely girlfriend, Sophia Shepherd." He greeted both of them. Sophia always hated it when someone declared he was her boyfriend, but she couldn't figure out why she felt that way. "Please have a seat," the man said. "I should introduce myself, Ms. Shepherd, I'm Francois Chevreau, and am in charge of a new venture that will expand the modeling industry around the world, especially in places like Africa and South America. That's why we're here."

"Sounds interesting," was all Sophia could muster.

Franklin and Sophia joined Francois at a table where several other men and women sat. Once they all were introduced, they started talking freely. Francois, who sat next to Sophia, asked her about her life as a model.

"It does get hectic with all the shows, but there's also this adrenaline rush I get when I walk down the runway."

Franklin interrupted. "And she does it superbly."

"I can imagine," Francois said. He turned back to Sophia. "How are Nathan and Ophelia doing?"

Her eyes jetted up as she took a drink of her wine. "You know my parents?"

"I surely do. They've traveled to Paris several times to meet with car dealers here about possibly bringing French cars back to the states. I've set up meetings for them. It hasn't happened, but they still continue trying."

"That would be my parents."

After he sipped his wine, Francois studied her. "How's Willis? Is he still dating that young girl, Allison, I believe?"

How did this man know so much about her? "They're still together as far as I know. I'll find out in a week, since I'm flying back to spend Thanksgiving and Christmas with them."

"That's exciting. Is Franklin joining you?"

Franklin took her arm. "I sure am."

It was close to eleven when Sophia and Franklin arrived back at the hotel. "That was a wonderful evening," he said, entering behind her. "I'm even more excited about tonight."

Sophia took a deep breath. "I'm tired. How about we call it a night."

He peered at her. "I'm not tired."

Sophia headed into the bathroom, and came back out in a few minutes dressed in a blue negligee.

"My favorite," he said, taking it off her. Minutes later Sophia stared at the ceiling listening to Franklin snore. He was satisfied, and that's all he cared about. Sophia wanted to get away from him, but her contract held her prisoner. She finally fell asleep, tears dotting her cheeks.

Chapter 3

When Chase returned from grabbing a drink, Dr. Boyd was still chatting with his mother. He had been talking to her since he arrived an hour ago and hadn't stopped. Chase turned to a kiss on the cheek by his sister, Samantha.

"Hey, little brother, how are things going?"

"Normal. Another case, and another night at the family's social event. This has to be the third one this week."

Samantha laughed. "You're a Connor, so you know how it works. Are you still thinking of getting out of the law field after only one year?"

"More and more each day. I don't know why I even got into it, but I did because the folks thought it would be good for me. Now I'm thinking about doing something different."

Samantha eyed him. "Have you talked to Mom and Dad about it?"

He sighed. "Doesn't do any good to tell them anything, since they have all the answers, but I'll talk to

Dad as soon as he's done with everyone else. I'm leaving with Dr. Boyd tomorrow, and we're going to Montana. Dr. Boyd and I had a conversation earlier this evening, and I've already told my boss about my plans. Of course, he wasn't too happy but he said he understood."

"Wow, you've always hated the cold. Why would you do a crazy thing like that?"

He grinned. "I hear it's pretty."

Samantha rolled her eyes. "That's a wonderful reason to move to Montana. You know I will miss you."

"And I'll miss you also," he said, hugging her. "Will you take care of my condo and everything associated with it? You can sell it if you want."

"Sure, I'll do that. I'll put it on the market and deposit the money into your account when it's sold. Is there anything else you need me to do?"

Chase thought for a moment. "I can't think of anything."

Samantha motioned with her head. "Now's your chance to tell Dad what you're up to. Here he comes. Good luck." Samantha slid out of the way when their father joined them.

"It's a wonderful party tonight, Chase, don't you think?"

"It is. It was good seeing Dr. Boyd also."

Oliver Connor eyed his son. "It sounds like he's moving onto something else. And my guess is he's talked to you about a job."

Chase grinned. "He did say something to you about it, didn't he?"

"He did," Oliver said. "When he first suggested

that he was heading to Montana, my first thought was he had asked you to join him, and I was ready to blow my stack, but I didn't. It's time you and all the kids make your own decisions, instead of your mother and I doing it for you."

"Are you my father?"

Oliver laughed. "Yeah, it makes you wonder after all these years, but I've seen you're not the attorney type. You do a wonderful job, but it's not you, and it's high time you find out who you are. If you plan to join Dr. Boyd, I'll let you out of your job commitment. If you find out it doesn't work, there'll be a job waiting for you when you return."

All Chase could say was, "thanks." After saying goodbye to his family, the next morning Chase and Dr. Boyd turned the vehicle toward Montana.

"I'm glad you're joining me in this trip," Dr. Boyd said. "It's more than a twenty-hour drive to Montana, but it will be a beautiful drive."

On the third day, Chase and Dr. Boyd crossed the Idaho state line into Montana. It had been snowing all day, something Chase wasn't used to. Chase pulled over off the side of the road when he saw a deer-like animal preparing to cross the interstate. Several cars had already stopped in the other lanes as well as the cars behind them. Rolling his window down, he grabbed his cell phone, and snapped some photos of the animal crossing the highway. Chase didn't know much about wild animals in Montana, so he turned to Dr. Boyd. "Is that an elk?"

He nodded. "It's a beautiful creature with reddish-brown in color. He's staring at us with his large, expressive eyes."

At one point the elk stopped right in front of his vehicle, surveyed the area, then continued across the road. Once the elk headed up into the mountains, Chase started moving the Jeep Cherokee forward. It was after dark when they arrived in Mountain Ridge, population 6,003 people.

Dr. Boyd pointed at a lit-up billboard on the side of the road. "Let's grab a bite to eat before we head to my house."

Chase drove downtown, noticing an antique shop, a bookstore, and a newspaper office.

Dr. Boyd pointed to the Mountain Ridge Bar & Grill. Chase pulled into a parking space a block down from the bar and grill. Both climbed out of the Jeep. Dr. Boyd rubbed his hands together. "It gets busy around here on Friday night, actually most nights."

Chase stopped and stared at the wooden sign that said Mountain Ridge Bar & Grill, framed with painted light rocks. Entering the bar and grill, he noticed a row of stools lining the bar and square wooden tables that had either two or four wooden seats. A large television screen over the bar was showing a hockey game, and several photos of Montana landscape adorned the walls of the room. He noticed a specific photo from Smith Lake of a couple of guys fishing off a small boat.

An older lady hurried over to them. "Find a place to sit, and I'll be right with you."

They found a booth back in the corner.

The blonde-haired lady set menus on the table. "I'll be back in a few minutes to grab your order. The special today is lasagna and breadsticks."

Dr. Boyd glanced at Chase and he nodded. He turned back to the host. "No need for a menu, we'll take

the special with water."
        "Coming right up."

Chapter 4

As the plane landed in the Kalispell airport Saturday afternoon, Franklin took Sophia's hand. "I bet you're glad to be back in Montana."

She turned to him. "I miss my home immensely, and I want to stay here, so I hope we can work something out."

He frowned. "We've talked about it, and I can't see a way out of your contract for another two years. Besides, you make heads turn when you strut down the runway, and look at the money you bring in."

All he thought about was her body. What had she done becoming a fashion model?

Once the plane landed at the gate, the two ambled out to the terminal and grabbed their bags. There waiting was her mother, Ophelia, with her short brown hair, manicured fingers, and tons of makeup. The two hugged each other.

"It's so good to see you, Mom. Of course, you know Franklin, my manager." Sophia didn't want to say boyfriend, since she didn't feel that way about him.

Her mom offered her hand. "Nice to meet you,

Franklin. We have a wonderful evening planned for you two. A good portion of people in town will be at our party to see our daughter. You're a popular gal in this region being a model."

Sophia sighed. "Mom, I hoped we could just keep it low-key. I just flew back from Paris."

Ophelia hugged her daughter. "You know better than that. Your father would never let an opportunity slip by to highlight a member of the family."

Sophia sighed. "That's true."

After packing their bags in the trunk and climbing into the car, they arrived at the mansion thirty minutes later at close to five. A short, stocky man with a cut beard opened the door for them. "Ms. Shepherd, it's wonderful to see you again."

She hugged the little man. "Wade, you're still working here for my parents? I'm surprised." She grinned at him, both knowing she was joking.

He blushed a bit. "They keep me around, but I'm glad I could see you. You're still a beautiful gal."

"Thanks. This is my manager, Franklin."

Franklin nodded at the guy. Wade turned to Ophelia's voice. "Take their baggage up to Sophia's room."

"Will do, ma'am."

Ophelia turned to Sophia and Franklin. "I hope that's okay with you two."

Franklin smiled. "Just perfect."

Ophelia took the man's arm and turned to Sophia. "I like this guy. Is there something you're not telling me?"

Sophia sighed. "No, Mom. He's my manager, and that's the extent of it."

Ophelia frowned. "I made a mistake, dear. I'll have Wade put his baggage in one of the guest rooms. Why didn't you say something earlier?"

"You really didn't give me a chance."

Franklin pulled Sophia aside. "We are together. What is this about?"

"Not now. I'm not sure how my father will handle the age difference."

When they entered the living room, there stood her father, with nicely combed blond hair, close-shaved face, and wearing glasses, along with her brother, who was a younger version of their father. Sophia introduced them. "This is my father, Nathan, and my brother, Willis."

Franklin proffered his hand to Nathan. "I've been so excited about meeting you, Mr. Shepherd. I've read and heard so much about your accomplishments."

Nathan grabbed his hand. "Well thank you, Franklin. You've done a wonderful job with my daughter and the money she's made as a model." Nathan turned to his daughter and hugged her. "How was Paris?"

She hugged him back. "It was wonderful as always. I'm glad to be back home for a bit."

"How long are you staying?" Willis asked.

"Through the first of the year. Franklin has to leave after Thanksgiving, but he wanted to join me for a bit to see where I grew up—"

Franklin interrupted. "And I'm happily surprised at what I see here."

Wade joined them. "Ms. Shepherd, your baggage is in your room."

"Thanks, Wade," she said.

Ophelia joined them. "In about an hour, the guests will start arriving, many of them clamoring to see our resident fashion model."

Sophia smiled at her mother. "I'm going to go upstairs to change into something more appropriate." She turned to Wade. "Will you please show Mr. Arthur to his room?"

"I will, Ms. Shepherd. It's so good to see you."

Sophia hurried upstairs to her room, shut the door, and fell down on the bed. She needed this break from everyone and everything. All she had wanted was to just relax in Montana, but she should have known better that her folks wouldn't allow it. They were proud of her, or at least that was the impression they gave everyone. She knew better. It was all about showing off their daughter.

It was an hour before Sophia appeared at the top of the stairs, dressed in a strapless green dress with matching boots. The room of people looked up at her as she glided down the stairs and into the lounge area. She took a deep breath and mingled, as was expected of her. Sophia peered up to see her sister, Meredith, standing at the bar with her boyfriend, Nick. Meredith, who just turned twenty-four, also stood five-nine, but had blond hair and emerald eyes. She should have been the model because she was that pretty, but instead, she chose to be a nurse at the Mountain Ridge hospital.

She hurried over to her sister. "Sophia, it's great to see you." Meredith hugged her sister and turned to her boyfriend. "I'm sure Mom told you about Nick."

"She did," Sophia said, hugging Nick. "Meredith chose a handsome man."

He blushed. "She never told me how beautiful you

were, Sophia."

"I get that a lot. How is the nursing business?"

Meredith sipped her drink. "It's been busy with a lot more accidents showing up in the emergency room."

"You're working in the emergency room?"

Meredith nodded. "For the past three months. I volunteered for a six-month rotation to help out, but I actually enjoy it much more than the regular. Of course, Nick hates it because I don't get home until early in the morning."

"I can imagine," Sophia said.

Nick piped up. "Are you home for good?"

Sophia leaned her head close to the two of them. "I hope so."

An hour later, needing some air, Sophia put on her coat, deciding to stroll out to the backyard near the pool area. The pool was covered now because of the snow, but she'd spent many hours in it when she was younger. She froze in her tracks when a movement at the poolside grabbed her attention. "Who are you?"

Chase peered up at her. "Who are you?"

"I asked you first."

Chase laughed. "I'm Chase. Now who are you?"

"Everybody knows who I am. I'm the talk of the social event tonight."

The man's eyebrows furrowed. "I'm sorry, ma'am, but I'm only here because Dr. Boyd asked me to join him. I have no idea who you are."

"My name is Sophia."

"Would you like to join me? I had to leave since it was getting pretty stuffy in there, all the people high on themselves."

This time Sophia couldn't help but laugh. "That's

why I'm out here too—to get a breath of fresh air. I take it you don't go to many of these things."

He rolled his eyes. "More than I care to."

She sat down across from him. "You're not from here, are you?"

"Nope, I just arrived last night with Dr. Boyd. We drove from California to Montana."

"Do you have a job here? I know Dr. Boyd is an attorney. Are you one?"

He nodded. "I am or was—I'm not sure at this point. That sounds confusing. Dr. Boyd asked me to join him in his law practice, but I'm not sure about it."

"Then why are you here?" Sophia asked, sipping her drink.

He ran his fingers through his hair. "He told me about a bookstore that was for sale, and I'm into books, so I thought I'd see about it."

"Mr. Boer is selling his bookstore? I didn't know that."

Chase peered up at her. "I don't know his name, but if he's the only bookstore owner, that would be him. Do you like books?"

She smiled for the first time. "I love to read."

He finally stood up. "You have a beautiful smile. I should get out of here before I go crazier than I am right now."

She frowned. "You're leaving?"

He nodded. "Like I said I'm only here for Dr. Boyd. He's in his element, so I'll just disappear and head back to the hotel."

"You're staying in a hotel?"

"Yes, until I find a place of my own; that is, if I decide to stick around."

She didn't know why she said it, but she did. "I hope you do."

Chapter 5

On Monday, while Dr. Boyd went to the law firm for work, Chase strolled to the bookstore two blocks down from the law firm. He arrived at ten to nine, viewed the sign saying it would open at nine-thirty, so he decided to check out the town.

He found a cafe where he stopped in to get a cup of coffee and a donut. While he was waiting in line, he noticed the young woman from Saturday night, Sophia, sitting with another gal who had blond hair. Sophia waved at him to join them.

After Chase grabbed his coffee and donut, he walked over to the women and stood over them. "You look much different than the other night."

Sophia grinned. "I don't wear dresses all the time."

"My guess is you'd look good in anything."

The other gal cleared her throat. "Sophia, what would Franklin think about you flirting?"

Before Sophia could respond, Chase jumped in. "Ma'am, I'm not flirting with her, and I have no idea who Franklin is. If he's in a relationship with Sophia, then he's a lucky man."

Sophia interrupted. "This is Allison. She's the girlfriend of my brother Willis."

"Nice to meet you, ma'am."

Allison nodded. "Why don't you join us?"

Chase eyed her. "If you're sure I'm not causing a problem, I'll join you."

Allison laughed. "No, I was just being protective of Sophia since Franklin's not here."

As Chase sat down, he spilled some of his coffee on the table. The gals picked up their food quickly. Chase smacked his head with the cuff of his hand. "I'm such a klutz." He hurried over to grab some more napkins, then returned to find the gals cleaning up the mess. "Thank you," he said.

Sophia grinned. "Are you always this way?"

He sighed. "At times I am. I'm sorry if I ruined your meal."

Sophia shook her head. "We're fine. Now maybe you can join us."

Chase sipped on his coffee. "Who's Franklin?"

Allison was getting ready to reply, but Sophia intervened. "He's a guy we both know."

Allison turned to stare at her then uttered, "Ouch." She peered down at her leg, then gave Sophia a quizzical look.

"Oh," Chase said. "Did you enjoy that party Saturday night?"

Sophia nodded. "There were quite a lot of people there. What did you think, Allison?"

"It was interesting, considering the guest of honor stepped out, and everyone was searching for her."

Sophia gently slapped her hand on the table. "That was rude that the guest of honor would do that. I'm sure everything went well."

Chase noticed the large clock. "Oh shoot, I've got to go."

Sophia's eyes widened. "Is anything wrong?"

He stood up. "No, I was supposed to meet the owner at the bookstore this morning when it opened, and it's almost nine-thirty."

Chase started to hurry away but scrambled back to grab his coffee, then he rushed out the door. Moments later, he hurried back in. "Sorry, I forgot to throw my garbage away. You two have a wonderful day." He noticed Sophia's grin as he rushed off.

Chase arrived at the bookstore just as a man opened it. "Good morning, sir."

The guy turned toward Chase. "Yes, young man?"

"I'm here to talk to you about the bookstore."

He smiled at Chase. "Ah, Chase Connor. Boyd told me that you may be interested. Please join me. It's wonderful to meet you."

The two walked into the bookstore. Chase's eyes took in the whole view—Wall-to-wall bookshelves, some barely full and some devoid of books.

The man noticed him staring. "Mr. Connor, it's not as many books as I would have liked, but I still have hope. Why don't you join me for some hot cocoa?"

"Sounds good."

The two sat at a small table by the display window where he could keep an eye on things. "My name is Tony Boer, and I've owned this bookstore for the past ten years."

"Dr. Boyd said you were planning to sell it. May I ask why?"

He held his hot chocolate with both hands. "I'm

ready to get out of this wintry weather, which is not good for my lung problems. The doctor suggested it would be better to move to a desert climate, so that's where I'm heading, as soon as I can find someone to buy this place. That may be difficult."

Chase sipped his cocoa. "This is very good."

"Thank you. Why are you interested?"

Chase crossed his arms. "I was an attorney in California and wanted to get out of the hubbub. Dr. Boyd told me about this bookstore for sale, so I thought why not? Dr. Boyd was my professor at Stanford University. I've spent the last year working at a major law firm in California."

Mr. Boer stared at Chase. "You'd quit a lucrative job in a law firm to take over a bookstore? I don't mean any disrespect, but are you crazy?"

Chase grinned. "You could say that, I guess, but I want some peace and quiet, not working eighty hours a week, hustling around in Los Angeles to solve cases. Dr. Boyd did offer me a job with his law firm here, but I decided to try something else."

"Do you know anything about running a bookstore?"

Chase finished his cocoa. "I love to read books, so that's a start."

Mr. Boer grinned. "Yes, that is a start." He showed Chase around the bookstore. "I have sixteen bookcases that hold at least five hundred books on them, but as you can tell, they're not all full, and you can also tell they are different colored bookcases. My grand plan was to paint them all in a brownish, rustic color that fits the antique nature of the building, but that hasn't happened yet."

Chase grabbed a book off the shelf. "Wow, this is a rare book. How did you acquire this?" he asked, placing the book back on the shelf.

Mr. Boer wiped his nose with a handkerchief. "I buy these old tomes from various dealers. However, as is the case with the main bookstores, I purchase most of my books from wholesalers. I also have a direct relationship with several publishers. I order books directly from them, which allows me to keep an inventory based on local preferences and community interests." He took a sip of his drink and continued. "I also support local authors by selling their published books on consignment. This means the bookstore displays the books, and the author receives sixty percent of the sales when a copy is sold."

"How has that worked?" Chase asked.

"Actually, fairly good for the four local authors that I have. I receive many donations of books to the bookstore, as well as visiting auctions and rummage sales around the area. Through these I'm able to have access to titles that might not otherwise be available."

Chase finished sipping his cocoa and set the cup down on a table. "It sounds like it takes a lot of work to gather the books necessary to keep the bookstore running smoothly. What about profits?"

Mr. Boer thought for a moment. "I'd say around three percent annually. Having said that, I realize it's not a lot, but the bookstore can thrive and turn a profit. For instance, the bookstore is often a community hub for hosting events—book clubs, author signings, and workshops. I've done a couple, but I sure could do more. The events actually do fairly well since people purchase books and pay a small fee for the workshops."

Mr. Boer covered his mouth and coughed. "I collaborate with the coffee shop and antique shop with joint promotions and cross-marketing, which benefits all parties. I was in the process of adapting to the changing times by embracing e-commerce, offering online ordering, and implementing curbside pickup, which, as you can imagine, was important during the pandemic.

"Finally, I've endeavored to create a small-town bookstore that retains historical elements by preserving antique shelves, maintaining original architecture, and celebrating the community's unique stories. I'm a bit behind on that, but a younger man like yourself would be able to do something like that, and you would have help from the community."

Chase rubbed his temple. "That's a lot to think about."

"Don't think too long because I may sell it soon."

Chase peered into Mr. Boer's eyes and grinned. "Do you have any others thinking about it?"

He lowered his eyes. "I wish I could say I did."

Chase patted his shoulder. "Mr. Boer, I'm interested, so let's take a look at the numbers."

Mr. Boer's eyes popped up. "Are you serious?"

Chase sighed. "I am, but I don't know why, since I'm quite sure I won't make millions off it, but it's not necessarily about the money. It's more about the importance the bookstore has in the community. Back in California, I've even seen businesses in large communities close, and I sure wouldn't want that to happen here."

Mr. Boer grabbed Chase's cup, carried it out to the kitchen, and walked back out. "Let's talk numbers over lunch. It is about twelve-thirty. I frequent the Mountain Ridge Bar & Grill, so I hope that's okay."

"They have good food, so that works for me."

Mr. Boer put up an "Out to Lunch" sign, then locked the door, and the two strolled toward the bar and grill. Chase opened the door for Mr. Boer, and the two walked in, searching for a place to sit. Chase motioned toward a table in the corner, and the two headed in that direction.

Once seated, the server joined them. "The special today is beef stew and biscuits."

Mr. Boer nodded he'd have that. "With a beer," he said.

Chase peered at the menu, then said, "I'll have the special also, with an iced tea."

After she left, Mr. Boer grinned. "I probably drink a bit too much, and that doesn't help my lungs." Mr. Boer pulled out a small pad from his pocket. "Let's do some figuring on what this would cost for you."

Chase took a deep breath. "You haven't thought about it?"

"I have, but I don't have anything down on paper at this point, since I really didn't think anyone would even consider buying it. Let's start with the overhead, which is low for me. I have two employees, both part-time high school students who come in after school for a few hours." He sipped on his water. "As you can imagine, the primary cost is retail space. Then there's inventory. Since I have people who donate books, I'm able to resell them, and the profit margins are excellent. One thing I don't have is e-commerce sales, but if I did, that would allow me to offer them to a broader market."

Mr. Boer smiled when the server brought him his

beer. "Another thing that bookstores are doing, but I haven't started, is complementary services. For instance, a small coffee shop in the building would draw customers, but I don't want to take profits away from other Mountain Ridge businesses." After he tasted his beer, Mr. Boer grinned. "One other thing, margins on new books are often less than five percent, so acquiring used books for free and reselling them is better for margins, but it requires considerable time investment."

Chase had another thought. "Do you rent the building, and is there an option to buy the building? What about upstairs?"

"I've never been upstairs, but I do rent downstairs for five hundred a month. I'm not sure about buying the building. You'd have to talk to the realtor."

They both stopped when their food was served. During that time Chase perused the restaurant and saw Sophia sitting with an older man. She noticed him, smiled, and waved. He returned the favor. Chase turned to Mr. Boer. "I'm willing to give the owner one hundred fifty grand if I can buy the place."

The old man's eyes widened. "That's a generous offer. I'll have Bobby Hamilton, the realtor, draw up the legal documents, but you should talk to him yourself. You might want to talk to Mr. Harper, who owns the antique shop next door. He's also interested in getting out of the business."

"I'll think about it."

Once they finished their meal, both went their separate ways. Chase stopped by Sophia's table. "Hi, Sophia."

They both glanced up. "How are you, Chase?" she

said.

"This must be your father."

Franklin growled. Sophia sighed. "This is my manager, Franklin Arthur."

"Manager? Wow, I was mistaken. I'm sorry about that."

Chapter 6

Once Chase left, Franklin glared at Sophia. "What has gotten into you? Ever since we've been here, you've made it seem like I'm not part of your life. We have been lovers for the past five years, and the last couple of years we've become closer."

Sophia wiped her mouth. "No, you've believed we've gotten closer. At times I feel like I'm just your plaything, walking the runway, then spending the night with you at your whim. For instance, I told you I was tired last night in Paris, and you didn't care. I'm not your whore."

"I've never treated you like that. You seem to enjoy spending time with me, especially at night."

Sophia took a deep breath knowing this conversation was going nowhere. "Let's just drop it."

Franklin grabbed her hands. "No, we're not letting it go. There is something going on with you, and I want to know what it is."

Sophia glared at him. "Right here in public? Don't you think our private life should be discussed in private, but if you want to discuss it right now, we will." She took a sip of her iced tea to reinforce her nerves. "I've been working for you since my seventeenth birthday, and I've done everything you've asked of me and more. I've brought in millions of dollars for you, but I'm treated with such disrespect. For that reason alone, I want out of the contract."

He took a deep breath. "Let's take a step back and see if there's something we can do about it. Is that fair?"

Sophia shook her head. "You're not hearing me. I want out of this life, and I want to start a new one."

"Without me?"

She set her fork down. "When we were first together, I cared a lot about you and hoped we could make something out of a life together, but over the last couple of years, that has changed. I don't want to be with you anymore, and the reason boils down to how you treat me. We're through."

Franklin was silent for a long moment. "You have two years left on your contract, and the only way you'll get out of the contract is to buy your way out of it."

"How much would that cost?"

He smiled. "Half a million dollars."

Anger filled her. "You know I don't have that kind of money, and even if I did, I wouldn't pay you that amount."

He shrugged. "That's what it'll cost to get out of your contract. Your father will do it for you, but he's the one who believes you should continue walking down runways because of the money you make." He started to pick up his drink but stopped. "Another way would be for you and me to get married while we're here."

She glared at him once more. "You're a real jerk. That will never happen."

He smiled once more. "Then you'll have to produce the money. That's the only way out." Franklin wiped his mouth with his napkin. "I'll give you until the end of the year. If I don't get the money, you'll be mine for two more years, and believe me, I'll enjoy our time together." He stood up. "I have to go. Your father asked me to join him, so he can show me around the car dealership. He's interested in me starting a car dealership in Denver. It sounds quite interesting." He reached over and kissed her on the cheek. She wiped it off. "Now, now, is that anyway to treat your manager and future husband? Your father may be interested in that arrangement despite our age difference. You see, it doesn't matter to him about age difference as long as he is happy with the husband you choose."

Once he left, Sophia slammed her fist down on the table. Many people stared her way. She shrugged. "Guess I drank my iced tea too quickly, and it went down the wrong way." Sophia sat there for a few minutes until the server brought over the bill. "Ugh," she said to herself. Franklin didn't even pay the bill. She gave the server her credit card with a fifteen percent tip. After she signed the receipt and took the slip, she headed out of the restaurant. Sophia hopped into her car and drove to Smith Lake where she could regroup. She was in a tight fix and had no idea how to get out of it on her own. Then she made a decision.

She drove by the attorney's office, stopped, and pulled into a parking spot. It was time to check on her legal rights. She got out and walked into his office.

A gal she knew sat at the front desk. "Sophia, I

heard you're in town. What are you doing here?"

"Is Dr. Boyd available?"

She smiled at Sophia. "He is. Please have a seat, and I'll ring him."

Sophia grabbed a seat and started reading an article in *People* magazine. Five minutes later, Dr. Boyd joined her.

"Sophia, what brings you to my office?"

"Dr. Boyd, I need to talk to you. I'm in a fix and don't know what to do."

"Come on back." He directed her into his office. "It's a little messy right now since we're just getting started." He picked up some books from a chair and set them on the floor beside his desk. "You can sit here."

"Thanks, Dr. Boyd."

"Please call me Darren," he said, pulling a chair around to sit facing her. "Now, what seems to be the problem?"

She took a deep breath. "You know I'm a fashion model, right?" Dr. Boyd nodded. She continued. "To get right to the point, I want to get out of my contract, but my manager is telling me I still have two years left on it."

Darren peered at her. "Did you talk to your manager about it?"

"Yes, he said if I paid him half a million dollars, he'd let me out of it, or I could marry him. I'll do neither."

He leaned forward on his elbows. "I don't blame you. Have you talked to your father about buying out the contract?"

She shook her head. "That won't happen. He's so adamant about the money that comes in from modeling, which is usually six figures."

Darren rubbed his chin. "That's a lot of money. I should step back and ask you why you want to get out of the business."

She sighed. "Simple, when I started, it was glamorous, but now it's just a headache and very stressful."

He reached back to grab a book. "Have you ever heard of the word, *unconscionability*?"

She shook her head.

He took a deep breath. "Right, and why would you? If a contract is extremely unfair or one-sided, it may be considered unconscionable. Courts may allow you to get out of the contract, especially if you were at a significant disadvantage during the negotiation process. Weren't you seventeen when it happened?"

"I had just turned seventeen. My father had offered to provide me with an attorney, but I wanted to do it myself."

"The court may find that it was a one-sided affair, since you were a minor."

Sophia shook her head. "My dad has an in with the judges in this county, and he wants me to continue modeling, so basically I'm stuck for the next two years."

"I'd need a copy of the contract. Do you have it?"

She hadn't thought about that. "I'm just here for a few days, although I'd like to stay. There's probably an online copy in my files. I'll send it to you."

He stood. "Let me have a look at it, and I'll get back to you."

After chatting for a few more minutes, Sophia walked out of the law office. She had just stepped out onto the sidewalk when her cell phone rang. Her father. She let it go to voicemail and then accidentally dropped her cell phone onto the sidewalk. "Damn it." She reached down and picked it up.

"I thought I was the only person who was klutzy."

She peered up at a tall man with blond hair and green eyes. "Can I help you?"

He grinned. "I thought I could help you by leaning down to pick up your cell phone, but you already have done that. I'm Kirby Hall."

She sighed. "Nice to meet you, Kirby Hall. My name is Sophia Shepherd."

He nodded. "I knew that, or I should say I've met your father, Nathan, and brother, Willis, who mentioned your name."

"Now why would they do that?" Sophia cast an eye at him.

"I'm not sure, but they did. I was talking to Willis about an incident at the Mountain Ridge Bar & Grill the other night. He saw an altercation between two gentlemen."

"You're a police officer?"

"I'm actually a detective with the Flathead County Sheriff's Department."

"I haven't seen you around, and our family knows almost all of the members of the sheriff's department."

He rubbed his jaw. "I'm new to the area. Just arrived three months ago."

She grinned. "And you're already involved with my family. I hope it wasn't too inconvenient."

He laughed. "Just a little awkward, since it seems your father does all the talking while your brother just follows along."

This time Sophia laughed. "You've truly met my father and brother."

"You have a beautiful laugh." At his comment, her face hardened. "What did I say?" he asked.

"I'm not in the mood for a guy to hit on me."

"Sorry if you believe I'm doing that, but I was just complimenting you. I should get going."
He started to walk away, but he turned when she touched his arm.

"I'm sorry. It's just been a difficult day."

"How about we grab a cup of coffee and we can talk about it?"

She eyed him. "Can detectives have coffee with civilians?"

He grinned. "I'm not working on a case that involves you, so yes, it's okay. Besides I'm off today."

The two walked over to a cafe around the corner. After they grabbed their lattes, they sat down at a table in a corner. "I remember seeing an older guy standing in the background with your father and brother. Is he someone of significance?"

Sophia sighed. "He's my manager, and for a time, he was more than that—until recently."

"Oh, got it. He doesn't want you to break it off with him, and he's also making it difficult as your manager."

She nodded. "Back when I was seventeen, we were close because I was infatuated with being with an older man, but now I've changed, and I don't want to be with him. I'm trying to find a way out of this whole modeling situation, but it's just not working. Seems I'll be stuck for another two years."

He patted her hands. "If you think negatively, it will happen. All you have to do is buy your boyfriend out or marry him."

Her mouth dropped. "How would you know something like that?"

"Where I come from in California, I've seen it all. I've covered several cases where a seventeen-year-old girl hooks up with a rich guy, but she won't press charges, or the parents of the rich guy find a way around the system. It's a crime to have sex with anyone under eighteen in the state."

"Is that why you're here?"

Kirby took a deep breath. "Yeah, I found out about a guy who spent the night with a seventeen-year-old girl at one of the many parties that the college campuses have. Her friend mentioned something about it, but the gal wouldn't say anything at all, so we didn't have a case."

"That's too bad. I take it the guy was rich?"

"Rich as they come. I decided to get away from all of that and was hired here."

Sophia sighed. "That's what I'm trying to do also."

"The guy looked much older than you were. Are you two married?"

"Oh gosh no, I had thought about it when I was seventeen, but not now. I just want to get away from him and it all."

"Marriage seems out of the question, so buy him out."

"Now you tell me." She grinned. "Where were you when I was seventeen?"

They both laughed.

"This was fun," Sophia said. "I'd like to do this again with you, if you have time."

He smiled. "I'd be delighted. How about I pick you

up for dinner tonight? It is Friday night, and I understand the bar and grill has wonderful specials, plus dancing. I can't remember the last time I danced."

"It's a date."

Chapter 7

Chase strolled down to the realtor's office three blocks from the bookstore. He opened the door and walked in. Sitting behind a desk was a white-haired guy with long hair tied in a ponytail. The guy looked up and reached out his hand. "I'm Bobby Hamilton. What can I do for you?"

Chase spoke up. "I'm interested in buying the bookstore."

He looked surprised. "Wonderful. Boer has been trying to sell it. How can I help?"

Chase rubbed his hands together. "He told me he rents from you, but I'd like to buy the whole building to run the bookstore downstairs and fix up the upstairs. Would you be interested, and how much would it cost?"

Hamilton grabbed some paperwork. "Yes, I'd be interested in selling the property. I have the listing right here. In fact, I understand Mr. Harper is interested in selling his antique shop, which is right next door, and if you can work out an arrangement with him, I'd give you a discount for both buildings."

"I'll talk to Mr. Harper."

"The building you are interested in is two stories and has 500 square feet on the bottom floor and 600 fifty square feet on the top floor for a total of 1150 square feet. And at 30 dollars per square foot, that comes out to close to 34,000 dollars. I'll sell it to you for 30,000 dollars, plus you'll have to cover all the extra expenses, so it could be between 40,000 to 50,000 dollars. If that interests you, I'll take care of all the paperwork."

Once that was completed, Chase stepped out into the street as the snow started to fall. He peered toward the north. The dark clouds were rolling in. He was going to experience his first blizzard today. He'd stop at the antique shop, then he would talk to Mr. Boer about what had just happened and check out the top floor.

He prepared to walk into the antique shop when three children flew past him. "I'm so sorry," a lady with black hair said, scurrying after the children into the store. Chase entered and noticed the three kids talking up a storm with a man in a wheelchair.

The harried young woman stood nearby. "Okay, you three, let your grandfather have a breath of fresh air." When the youngsters stepped back from the man, she said, "That's better."

The old man grinned at the young lady. "Laci, calm down, they have a lot of energy."

"Dad, they need to show respect in a business."

Laci and the old man turned toward Chase who was browsing at a shelf of antiques by the door. The man in the wheelchair rolled over to him. "Welcome to the antique shop. Anything specific you're searching for?"

Chase's eyes took in the whole place. "You have a

wide assortment here— furniture, tools, Old West memorabilia, and paintings, to name a few."

A screechy voice from the backroom hollered, "Harold, are you ready for biscuits?"

Harold switched his head to Chase. "Nag. Nag."

They turned to a woman belonging to the voice. "Go ahead and laugh," said the lady, who looked like an older version of the one named Laci. "I know you want to."

Chase turned to Harold. "She seems like a nice woman."

Harold laughed. "My wife has purplish gray hair. Tell me who at sixty-one would have that color of hair—"

Laci interrupted. "Mom, Dad, calm down and quit scaring away the customers with your antics."

The lady with purple hair offered her hand. "I'm Valeria, this is my grumpy husband, Harold, our daughter, Laci, and those three rascals are her children."

"Nice to meet you all," Chase said.

Valeria pulled out a couple of chairs and set them around a table. "Have a seat and let's talk. I'll make us some coffee, and I also have some freshly baked biscuits to go with it."

Chase had taken a seat on one of the chairs when Valeria came out five minutes later with coffee cups, coffee, and biscuits.

Laci ran to meet her mom. "I can help."

The four sat down around the old round table that appeared to have one leg ready to fall off.

Valeria studied Chase as she buttered a biscuit. "What brings you here?"

"I'm interested in purchasing the antique store. I hear it's for sale."

"Do you know anything about antiques?"

"Not a lot, but then I know nothing about operating a bookstore, and Mr. Boer sold it to me," Chase said. "By definition, an antique shop is a retail shop specializing in the sale of antiques, but in my mind, it's much more than that."

Harold sipped on his coffee. "There are many reasons to buy antiques or vintage items, if you want to call them that, but three reasons stick out — thrift, value, and an appreciation for quality. In addition, antiques allow us to rediscover parts of our past, including things we would have never expected."

Valeria finished her biscuit. "Antique sales have changed over the years, especially with the introduction of online antique shops. We've tried to go that way also, but we're not the technological geeks that many others are, so we're behind everyone else. Most of our inventory comes from auctions, estate sales, flea markets, and garage sales. But as you get older, it gets tougher to frequent those places."

Harold agreed. "Again, as my wife said, it's getting tough to reach the places that have the inventory, and then there's always marketing. That's why we're ready to close up shop or hopefully find a buyer. At the end of the day, it's still a business, and we'd like to recoup something for our efforts over the years."

Chase stood up and handed them a card. "You think about it and contact me if you're interested in selling. I'm at the local hotel. You can leave a message and I'll get back to you."

Harold took his hand and shook it. "I'll be in

touch."

Chase stepped outside and started to turn into the bookstore when Sophia and Detective Hall stepped out of the building they were in, almost bumping into him. "Chase, good morning."

Chase eyed Detective Hall but turned toward Sophia. "Good morning, Sophia. And you too, Detective Hall. "Sophia peered at the two. "You two know each other?"

Chase responded, "We're both from LA. He also wanted to get away from all that sun and traffic."

Kirby narrowed his eyes toward Chase. "Some of us had no choice."

Sophia's eyes flitted from one to the other. Then she said to Kirby, "I should get going. I'll see you tonight."

He smiled. "I'll pick you up at six."

"I'll be ready."

Once Sophia left, Kirby turned toward Chase. "How are things going with you?"

"I'm in the process of purchasing a bookstore."

Kirby's eyes lifted. "A bookstore. You're throwing away a lucrative career with your father as an attorney?"

Chase sighed. "Saw too many people get off for crimes they'd committed simply because they had money, or someone was afraid to tell the truth."

Kirby grinned. "I ran into that in California once or twice myself."

Chase stuffed his hands in his pockets. "I should get going. Have to meet a guy about a building."

When Kirby didn't respond, Chase stared at the detective. "I'm not that same guy."

Ten minutes later, he walked into the bookstore and waved at Tony, who was dusting something behind the counter.

The old man glanced over his shoulder. "Good to see you again, Chase. What's up?"

"Mr. Hamilton is selling me the building, which means if we can come to an agreement, you'll be making your way to somewhere warm real soon."

"That is wonderful news," he said. "I'll get the paperwork for the sale of the business at the price we agreed upon."

"Great, do you mind if I check upstairs?" Chase asked.

"No, go ahead."

Chase climbed the stairs to find a closed door. He opened it and entered the dark space. He searched for a light switch, found it, and flipped it on. A small apartment of sorts. Not too bad of a space, Chase thought. But it needs a lot of work.

He moseyed around the apartment. There was a small kitchen with a table and four chairs, three broken. At least one was safe. Chase smiled. The living room was fairly large. A nice couch would fit nicely right there by the wall.

When Chase opened the bathroom door, a bird took off making him duck. He reached over and shut the window in the bathroom. *What do you know? A bird decided to use the bathroom.* He walked into the bedroom. It was spacious enough. He could put a king-sized bed in it, so he had room to roll over without falling off. Chase leaned against the door and surveyed the room. He could make it work.

He walked downstairs to see Mr. Boer selling

books to a customer. Once she was gone, he joined him. "Well, can you make it work?"

The old man offered him a broad smile. "I believe I can."

~

Sophia checked her watch again. Was Kirby going to be late? She smoothed her long blue dress and checked the mirror one last time. Sophia had to admit she was excited about tonight's date.

"You're all dressed up. What's going on?" Franklin walked in the room and gave her the once-over.

"I have a date tonight with someone other than you."

He glared at her. "Don't think this is over."

They both turned at the knock at the door. Sophia hurried over to answer it.

Kirby Hall stood in the hall, his eyes twinkling. "Wow, you look elegant," he said.

She smiled. "Thank you. This is Franklin, my manager."

Kirby eyed the guy. "Nice to meet you, Franklin."

"You too. Don't let Sophia fool you. She has a way of twisting things around in her favor."

Kirby's eyes narrowed. "I'm sure we'll be just fine." He turned to Sophia. "Should we go?"

"I'd love to." She placed her arm in his, the door closing behind her. Once at the car, he opened the car door for her and helped her in. She peered up at her hotel window and noticed Franklin glaring down at her. "I'm sorry about Franklin."

Kirby shook his head and started the car. "Don't be. I've dealt with guys like that many times."

She cast a sideways glance at him. "You are a young detective. How long have you been doing the job?"

"Not that young. I'm thirty, and I've been a detective for three years."

She took a deep breath. "I saw the tension between you and Chase. If you don't want to talk about it, we don't have to."

"It's okay. We just had an issue in California that was taken care of by his parents."

She peered at him and took a deep breath. "Chase was the guy who was with an underaged girl."

He nodded. "The girl wouldn't press charges; nor did she ever admit the two had a liaison together, so there was nothing we could do about it."

"How did you find out in the first place?"

"Her friend told us about it."

Sophia put her hands on her legs. "Couldn't you do something about that?"

"We could have, but the Connors were able to prove that the girlfriend was jealous that she couldn't hook up with Chase, so at the hearing, the judge dropped the case."

"And Chase got away with it?"

"He did. Enough about Chase Connor. Let's eat."

Once the two finished eating their dinner, he drove her back to the Shepherd household. She turned to face him. "Please come in and have a drink with me."

He eyed her. "That might not be a good idea."

Her eyes lit up. "You don't drink?"

He grinned. "It's just that you're awfully pretty, and I may not be able to control myself."

She blushed. "And you're handsome."

He started to climb out of the car. "Now that we have that settled, let's go have that drink."

They walked in to see Franklin waiting for them with a document. He handed her the contract. "I'm releasing you from your contract. Your daddy gave me one hundred thousand dollars." He grinned.

"So that's all you wanted was the money."

He touched her cheek. "Little girl, it's always been about money. Don't think any different. Anyway, enjoy your life up here in the cold wilderness."

Sophia watched as he walked out the door.

Five minutes later a shot rang out. Kirby and Sophia bolted out the door and scrambled down the stairs. A body lay in the street. They ran over to the body and saw Franklin. Sophia screamed, and others came flying out of the house.

"What happened?" Nathan asked, the first one on the scene.

Sophia was shaking. "I don't know. I heard a shot and found him lying on the street."

Nathan checked his pulse. "Call 9-1-1."

Willis, who was standing behind his father, dialed 9-1-1. Twenty minutes later the EMT arrived and went to work. One of them peered up at Nathan. "He's gone. He wasn't shot, but it appears he was hit by a car. It seems he was killed on impact."

Kirby peered up at her father. "We both heard a gunshot."

The county sheriff joined them. "Detective Hall, I'll take it from here. It would be best if you left the scene. Ms. Shepherd, can we talk?"

She nodded, watching as Kirby left the area. The sheriff sat down a few feet away from her. "I understand he was your manager and you two were together?"

"Yes, sir, but we had broken that off a few minutes before."

"Could you tell me why?"

She wrapped her arms around her body. "I'd wanted to get out of my contract for a long time. When I arrived back from dinner, Franklin handed me a new contract releasing me from the modeling agency, wished me well, then he left."

The county sheriff finished writing down his notes. "Was there anything during the evening out of the ordinary?"

She thought for a moment. "Nothing that I can remember."

"Anything associated with the deceased?"

"Not that I can think of."

He stood up. "That should do for now. If I have any more questions, I'll call you. If you think of anything, please call me."

After he left, she picked up her cell phone and dialed a number. "I'm scared."

Chapter 8

It was eight-thirty when Sophia walked into the Mountain Ridge Bar & Grill. Chase jumped up when he saw her and hurried over to her. "Are you okay?"

She explained what happened.

He held her hands. "Have you ever heard a shot from a gun before?"

She nodded. "My dad and brother go hunting all the time, and several times they have taken me with them."

"Do you think your father or brother did it?"

She sighed. "I can't answer that; I just know I can't stay in that house tonight. Can I stay with you?"

Chase eyed her. "Are you sure it'll be okay? I can see you're pretty emotional." He sighed. "The Boyds have a screened-in porch attached to the house. Dr. Boyd told me if I ever wanted to stay there it was okay. You can stay there."

The two climbed into his car, drove to the Boyds, and the two entered through the screen door. They sat down on the couch. "You can sleep here tonight,"

Chase said.

She shook her head. "Would you stay with me?"

He stared at her face devoid of color. "Yeah, I will. Would you like something to drink?"

"No, I'm good." She reached out her hand. "Can we just sit here for a bit?"

He sat down by her and put his arm around her.

"Thank you. I don't mean to be a burden, but the gunshot and seeing Franklin lying there in a puddle of blood scared me."

He gently stroked her hair. "Let's talk about something different."

Her eyes peered up at him and she grinned. "It's a nice little place."

He laughed. "Nothing like you live in."

She grinned. "You're right, my bedroom's larger than this room."

"Ugh," he said, as if he'd stuck a knife in his heart. "That cut deep."

She laughed. "Thank you, I needed that. There is something about you that makes me feel safe, and I've never felt that way. That's why I called you."

"I'm glad you did. Why don't you try to get some sleep."

She sighed. "I can't because I'm too wound up. Guess I'm also wondering what I'm going to do now that I'm out of a job. I've always just relied on my body—walking the runway. Is that what you think when you see me—just a body?"

Chase was in a tricky situation. "There are so many wonderful things about you. Take for instance your smile, which is one thing that attracted me to you. It's contagious, and I've seen the mood of those around you light up when you smile." He took a deep breath. "Then there's your eyes. They're sparkling emerald and beautiful. Anyone can see the emotions and moods they carry, be it joy, sadness, curiosity, or attraction. I've only seen joy and curiosity reflected in your eyes since I've known you."

She smiled. "Thank you. I needed that. Will you stay here with me?"

"Until you fall asleep."

She nudged into his chest and pulled the blanket over the two of them. "I hope you stay here all night with me."

~

The next morning Sophia had just walked through the front door of her family's house when Willis chased her down. "Where have you been?"

"I spent the night elsewhere. I just couldn't be in the house after what happened."

Willis put his arm around her. "Everyone was worried about you."

She smiled. "As you can see, I'm okay."

They turned to another voice. "Dear, thank God you're okay. We thought you had done something drastic after losing Franklin."

Sophia stared at Ophelia. "Mom, I'm okay."

"Where were you last night?"

She didn't want to tell her mother the truth. "Nothing earth-shattering, I found a room in a hotel, and I paid for it in cash. I needed to get away from everyone and everything that happened last night. It didn't help much because things don't add up."

"Like what?" Willis asked.

She took a deep breath. "I heard a gunshot, and

Franklin was lying on the street."

Nathan joined them. "Sweetie, a car that backfires can sound like a gunshot, and he may have still been breathing when you got there, but perhaps he was on his last breath. That's not that unusual."

Sophia hesitated. "I'm going to go upstairs to soak in the tub."

Nathan hugged his daughter. "You do that, then we'll go for a ride." Her eyes widened.

Ophelia smiled. "It's okay, dear. We plan to make you a partner in the car dealership business. There are some big plans ahead that our children are going to be part of."

Sophia peered at her mother. "Even if I'm not interested?"

"What would you be interested in?" Willis asked.

"Books."

Sophia sat in her bathtub soaking in the warm suds thinking about what her parents were planning. She wanted nothing to do with being a partner in a car dealership.

Her thoughts traveled to the new men in her life—Chase Connor and Kirby Hall. Two different guys. Chase could be charming as was evident last night when he talked about her eyes, her smile. He was so sweet, but she knew full well that he was attracted to her body, just like most guys. Still he'd talked about feelings. She could love a guy like that.

Kirby was also a guy she could fall in love with also. Her father would approve of Kirby Hall since he was a detective in the police force, and her dad had control over their leaders.

After she hopped out of the bathtub and put some

jeans and a sweater on, Sophia joined her father who waited for her in his office.

"Let's take a ride to talk about what I have in mind for you."

"Dad, I know what I want to do."

His eyes widened. "How can you know when you just got home and saw your boyfriend killed?"

"I met someone who interests me in every way possible." Actually, there were two men, but Sophia wouldn't say anything about Chase, ever.

He eyed his daughter. "That's awfully soon."

"Maybe we should go for a ride."

The two climbed into her father's Rolls Royce Phantom VII, which cost him almost five hundred grand, but he loved to flaunt his money, as did her mother and brother. They left Mountain Ridge, driving toward the north.

"Tell me about this guy you met."

Sophia stared out at the scenery whizzing past. "I just met him within the last week or so. I don't know him as well as I'd hope to, but I want to get to know him better, so I plan to date him. That's a first for me."

"What does he do?"

Sophia sighed. "Law enforcement."

Her father's face turned red. "How can you even think about someone who's in law enforcement?"

"Calm down. He's a good guy, and he'll do something special in his life, that I know. I thought you'd be happy for me."

He growled. "This is unacceptable. A Shepherd does not become involved with anyone who has no future."

This time Sophia was angry. "You have no idea

what he's capable of. The guy is starting his life over, which is fine, because that's what I'm doing also. You have no problem with me doing that. In addition, we both know that you have law enforcement under your thumb, so this should be a perfect match for me."

"The difference is I'm handing you something that will keep the Shepherd tradition going."

"Wow, so now you have to hand me something because I can't do anything on my own?"

Her father glared at her. "You left a six-figure job because you couldn't handle it."

Sophia clammed up to keep from saying something she'd regret later.

Her father continued. "Let's get this straight. You want to be with a guy who has no future for what reason? He's handsome? He's good in bed? What is it?"

Sophia glared at her father. "It's okay for a guy sixteen years older than me to be in my life, but someone I could truly care about—even possibly love—is wrong because he doesn't have a job that meets your standards?"

"Your destiny is in Denver, or you leave our family for good. That's the end of the conversation."

She took a deep breath but didn't say anything. Her father turned the vehicle around, then drove back to the house. Once he stopped in the driveway, Sophia slammed the door, hurried into the house, up the stairs, and into her room. She grabbed a suitcase and threw in clothes, as well as items important to her. Fifteen minutes later, she scrambled down the stairs to the living room.

Her mother stopped her. "What's this all about?"

Sophia pivoted toward her mother. "I'm tired of being treated like dirt by men in my life. I've found someone I want to be with, but good old Dad won't even think about me with a man in law enforcement because he doesn't meet his expectations."

Ophelia's mouth dropped. "Why would you want to be with a guy who's in that field? That's not the Shepherd way."

Sophia glared at her mother. "You too? Since I'm not going to Denver like your husband asked, he told me to leave this house for good. That's exactly what I'm doing. No issues. I'm out of here."

Chapter 9

Chase peered around Dr. Boyd's law office reception area for the tenth time. He checked his watch. "How long do you think this is going to take?"

Mr. Boer shrugged. "All we have to do is sign our names for transferring the bookstore from me to you. Shouldn't take long."

Chase turned to Mr. Boer. "When do you plan on heading south?"

"I have a couple of issues to finish over the next couple of days but hope to fly out by the weekend. I'm excited about all of this."

Chase took a sip of his coffee. "I am too, but I'm also a bit nervous, since I've never done anything like this. FYI, I plan to keep the part-time employees on for the time being."

Mr. Boer blew out a breath. "That's good news because they were scared they wouldn't have jobs after the business was sold. What are your first plans?"

"Wow, there are so many. I'm going to restore the bookcases to match the architecture of the building. At the same time, I'm going to renovate the upstairs, so I can move out of the hotel. There is a lot to do."

Mr. Boer placed his coffee on the table next to him. "Before I forget, there's a book-sales conference this weekend in Whitefish that you should attend. It occurs each year, which will be a good opportunity for you to meet other book sellers from around the state, the region, as well as the nation. They come from everywhere. I'm already signed up, plus hotel space is reserved for you for two nights."

"Thank you."

"I also have put together a list of various book sellers' conferences that would be good for you to consider attending around the region. There are also several conferences where you can purchase collectibles. The one I would suggest is in March in St. Petersburg, Florida, which features rare and collectible books."

They both turned to Dr. Boyd's voice. "Come on in, you two. Let's take care of business."

They walked into Dr. Boyd's scrunched office with a small desk, small table with two chairs, law books lining the walls, as well as a map of the county.

"Have a seat. Here are the documents you'll need to sign to complete the transfer of the bookstore from Mr. Boer to Mr. Connor. In addition, I also have documents to sign pertaining to the sale of the building to Mr. Connor. Mr. Hamilton couldn't make it today, so he asked me to handle it."

After thirty minutes of signing various documents, the property legally became Chase's. He provided a check to purchase the bookstore to Mr. Boer, plus a check to Dr. Boyd to purchase the building itself. Dr. Boyd double-checked everything, then ten minutes later, he peered up at the two. "The transaction is completed."

Mr. Boer hurried out the door with the check.

"He's in a hurry," Dr. Boyd observed.

Chase grinned. "He can't wait to move to a warmer climate."

Dr. Boyd ran his fingers through his hair. "Why don't you join my family for dinner tonight?"

"I think I will. What time?"

Dr. Boyd stood and pushed his chair in. "Six will be fine. I'll make sure to tell the wife you're coming. Will you be bringing that lovely Sophia Shepherd with you?"

Chase shook his head. "She's moved on to a detective."

Dr. Boyd put his coffee cup down. "That's her loss. She'll probably be moving to Denver to run her dad's new car dealership."

Chase released a breath. "I wouldn't blame her if she took the job." He stood. "I should get going. See you at six." It was snowing and the wind was blowing when he stepped out of the office. He pulled up his coat collar, then hurried the three blocks to the bookstore. Once he arrived, he placed the key into the door, opened it, and stepped in. He stood for a moment staring at the books on the shelves. This bookstore was now his. He had a lot of work to do to make it profitable.

He checked the clock on the wall seeing it was three-thirty. He would put ninety minutes of work into the bookstore before going to the hotel to change into clothes for his dinner engagement with Dr. Boyd. Chase thought about calling Sophia to see if she would like to join him but squelched the thought. Too many question marks to handle at the moment.

Chase put thoughts of Sophia on the backburner for the time being since he wanted to focus on unpacking the boxes of books onto the shelves. He inventoried the books, then carried them to the right shelves. He was able to make it through half a dozen boxes before he called it quits for the night, but then the front door opened. "Sorry, the bookstore is closed."

"I locked it and placed the closed sign on the window." A familiar female voice.

He walked to the entrance. "What are you doing here, Sophia?"

"I wanted to see how you were doing. I don't see you much, now that you're into the bookstore business." She grinned. "Are you enjoying it?"

"I am. It's tough trying to get everything together, but I'm getting there. How about you and Kirby?"

Her eyes peered into his. "We've gone out a couple of times but nothing serious. When are you going to ask me out?"

He frowned. "You're better off with Detective Hall." Chase finished what he was doing and stacked the empty boxes.

"Where are you heading to now?" Sophia asked.

"I have a dinner date with the Boyds."

She linked his arm into his. "Then it's a good thing I wore a nice dress."

"No, Sophia. You're a beautiful gal, but it would never work. I come with too much baggage."

She put her hands on her hips. "Wow, I've never been turned down like that before. Good luck on your new venture." She spun around and left the store.

Chase arrived at the Boyds' house just before six. A young girl with curly blonde hair greeted him at the door. "Chase, you did show up, but there's no girl with you. I always thought the Connors had gals lined up."

Chase rolled his eyes. "And you're only twelve, Clementine. What happens when you turn eighteen?"

She grinned. "Hopefully, you'll still be available."

She turned to her father's stern voice. "You know better."

"I'm sorry, Daddy." As Clementine skipped away, Dr. Boyd welcomed him in. "Twelve-year-olds who want to be eighteen. How do parents deal with it?"

They laughed. "Come on in. Mallory is almost done with supper." The doctor led him into the dining room and indicated where he should sit.

Mallory entered the room and started setting the food on the table.

Clementine joined them with a platter of roast beef. "I did the best I could by cutting the roast beef. I hope it's okay."

Mallory came behind her, placing her hand on Clementine's shoulder. "It'll be fine."

After they'd prayed and took their first bites, Chase turned to Mrs. Boyd. "Ma'am, this is exceptionally good. I can't remember tasting roast beef this moist. Thank you."

"You're welcome. It's been in the crockpot since ten this morning. I've found about eight hours is the best amount of time to cook a roast. Others may disagree."

"How is Kady doing? I haven't seen her in a couple of years."

Dr. Boyd smiled. "Our oldest daughter is doing

wonderful. She's engaged to a nice guy and they expect to be married in June. At least those are the plans at this moment. They may change."

Over the next hour, the group enjoyed their meal and chatted. Mallory mentioned the bookstore. "Darren told me you bought Mr. Boer's bookstore. Knowing who you are, I have to ask, what were you thinking?"

"Mallory," her husband uttered.

Chase laughed. "I ask myself the same question, but like I told your husband, I need to do something for myself, not what my parents want. If I fail, it's all on me. I can deal with that. In fact, I might purchase the antique store and combine the two."

Dr. Boyd peered up. "That would be a wonderful idea. They had talked about combining the businesses but could never agree upon anything. Hopefully, you can pull it off."

Chase changed the conversation. "If I remember right, the two Boyd gals are deadly in Monopoly."

Clementine grinned. "We are. Are you ready to lose all your money?"

Mallory jumped in. "Cleanup first." Dr. Boyd gawked at Clementine. She grinned at him. "It means more Monopoly."

Chapter 10

After spending a couple of hours at the bar and grill, Sophia walked into the house. She figured her father had calmed down a bit so they could talk about what had happened. That was the way he was. She walked into the living room where her father sat on the couch and sat beside him. "Are you calmed down a bit where we can talk?"

"You know me so well," he said, wrapping his arm around her. "Sweetie, I didn't handle anything right at all. I wouldn't blame you if you didn't want to speak to me at all, but I do have some things I want to talk to you about." He put on a smile. "Mountain Ridge is a small town. I want you to take over the Denver operation because you have so much potential, but after thinking about it, I confess I was wrong. You came out of a relationship that was not your choice. For that I'm sorry." He sipped on his coffee. "If you wish to be with the law enforcement officer, I'll support you one hundred percent. I want you to have your own life, and all I want is your happiness."

Sophia spoke for the first time. "I don't know if

he's the one I want, but I do know deep in my heart I want to do whatever I can to make the relationship work—one of my choosing."

He sighed. "What are you going to do now that you're back in Montana?"

Sophia peered up at her father. "I'm really not sure yet. I have a couple of ideas, but one of them isn't working for the company. I want to do it on my own."

"I'm proud to hear you say that. Realize I'll be there to help you no matter what it is."

She took his hands. "I always knew you would." Sophia took a deep breath. "How did you know Mom was the one for you?"

He sat back. "Wow, that's hard to explain. You just know that they're the person for you."

She grinned. "Maybe it would be better to talk to Mom about this."

He laughed. "You'd probably be right." Her father stood up and patted his daughter on the shoulder. "Are we okay?"

"Yes, we're okay, Dad. Please just let me handle my life. I have an idea where I want to go and who I want to be with, but it's going to take time."

~

When Chase arrived at the bookstore the next morning, a young man stood waiting for him at the locked door. "Can I help you?"

He smiled. "Sophia Shepherd suggested I stop by to help you with a computer programming system."

"That was awfully quick."

"She said it was important, so here I am."

Chase opened the door, and the two walked in.

"My name is James Leopold, and I handle the

computer equipment at Flathead Valley Community College."

"How do you know Sophia?"

"We dated for several months in high school, and we've been friends since."

Chase explained to him what he was looking for, particularly a more efficient system for handling books coming in and out, and for money exchanges. "While you're putting together the system, I'm going to stack books on the shelves."

As he was placing one of the larger historical books on the shelf, something hit him about the book. He climbed down off the ladder. Chase had a feeling something in the book was significant. He read the index, noticing the book was full of maps, as well as historical information about various areas. When the front door opened quickly, he put the book into a large drawer in his desk. "Can I help you?" he said, hurrying over to the customer.

"I was looking for some historical books. Mr. Boer used to have a collection."

Chase took him to the historical section. "Here's what we have. If you're looking for a specific title, please let me know. We may be able to order it."

He shook his head. "I don't know about the title of the book. Saw it once when I was younger, but my parents wouldn't buy it. It was a book about historical Montana, and I remember it was full of maps."

"Let's take a look." Chase handed him several older dusty books from the top shelves.

"No luck," the man finally said. "It's been like this everywhere I've gone."

"Why is that book so important?" Chase asked.

"I'm just into maps."

"Hold it, there are some old Montana maps over here in the reference section. Let's check them out. You'll find a map that fits what you're looking for."

"Good idea."

Chase spent the next half hour helping the man. He ended up purchasing three maps that were of significance to him. As they were walking toward the register, Chase asked, "What is it about these maps, other than they're old, that is important?"

He stopped and turned to him. "There are people who believe a certain map contains an ancient secret. I have no idea what that is, but there are people who will spend lots of money for it."

"Do you believe one of these maps is it?"

He shook his head. "I'm not sure what the map is that everybody is searching for, but these maps are also what I need for some class presentations. I'm a history professor at the University of Idaho."

One good thing about the gentleman purchasing the maps was that Chase was able to test out his new computer system. It worked perfectly.

That afternoon, a group of students entered the bookstore to browse through the stacks. Clementine Boyd was one of them.

She winked at Chase. "We had heard there may be some new books on sale here, so we thought we'd give it a try."

"Thanks."

She smiled and joined her friends. Several minutes later, Clementine came back her arms laden with several books. "Did you know that you have a couple of rare volumes in the bookstore?"

"Now how would you know that?"

"Our history teacher is a historical buff, and he's always telling us about these old books. I remember one in particular he was telling us about. Something to do with archaeological finds in Montana, which is one of the books you have. He might buy it from you for hundreds of dollars instead of ten."

Chase stared at her, his head tilted to the side.

"What?" she asked. "Despite what my folks believe, I do listen and pay attention in school. Did you know that there is a map that people have been searching for that can't be found?"

"I didn't know that."

"How can you run a bookstore if you don't know that?"

Chase laughed. "Good point. You're hired."

"For what?" her eyes lit up.

"When an old book comes in, you'll be responsible to do all the research you can on it and get back to me with any information you can."

She grinned. "I'm not cheap, but I will consider it."

"You do that and let me know. What's your history teacher's name?"

"Mr. Grant. He does nothing but study history. No family, nothing."

A middle-aged man in line behind Clementine spoke up, "The guy has the right idea. Marriage is for the birds."

Chase took his books. "Are these all of them?"

"You bet. I'll be back, since there are so many books to read. I never knew about this place; it's a golden gem in Mountain Ridge."

After the guy left, Chase peered at Clementine who

leaned against the counter, "How wouldn't he know this store was here?"

"Mr. Boer wasn't the kindest guy, so many times people would come in once or twice, then never come back. Of course being in a small town, they would pass it on about his nastiness."

"I'll remember to be nice."

Clementine took a deep breath. "That won't be hard for you since you've always been nice to my sister and me. I should get going. I'll let you know about the research job."

Once the girl left with her friends, a short, bald-headed man with a graying beard strolled in. "Looking for Chase. I was told he needed some estimates for a building project involving the upper part of the building."

"That's me. And you are?"

"Matt Leopold. My son was here earlier installing your computer system."

Chase laughed. "Sorry, but it's amazing how everyone knows everyone in small towns." He stuck his hand out. "Nice to meet you. Thanks for stopping by at such short notice."

Matt smiled. "You're new to the area, but you'll find out when there's something new, people will respond quickly. Sophia has been nice to my son, so it's the least I could do for her. Let's take a look at what you have."

The two climbed up the stairs. Chase opened the door at the top.

"What are your hopes for this?" Matt asked.

"I want to make it livable."

"Whew, it's going to take some money. Explain to

me what you're thinking."

Chase started with the kitchen area. "I'll need some new appliances, and I'd also like to lighten the background up a bit." Matt took some notes. They went to the living room. "I would like to put together an open concept in this area if possible. Maybe knock down a wall."

"A fireplace?"

"If it's possible, but it's not a must." The two walked into the main bedroom.

Matt eyed it. "This is larger than most master bedrooms. Is it possible it could have been two bedrooms?"

"That I can't answer, but it would be safe to say it was." They looked at the other bedroom, then finally the bathroom.

"Wow, this needs major refurbishing."

"I figured that," Chase said. "What are your thoughts?"

Matt tapped his chin. "Initially, it'll take several weeks plus close to hundred thousand dollars, if not more. I'll put together some blueprints with ideas for you to inspect. I should have that done early next week."

Chase had leaned against the wall. "Sounds good."

It was close to five when the bookstore would be closing. Once the guy left, Chase checked his cash register to see what he had made for the day. He finished counting at two hundred forty-seven dollars. Not bad, he thought, for a day's worth of used books.

After he placed the money into a night-drop bag, Chase strolled down to the bank, which was two blocks away. He dropped the bag into the night drop, stopped, and surveyed the area. Someone was following him.

~

"I think I found the book at the bookstore in Mountain Ridge."

"That's good news," the man said on the other end of the phone. "Is there any way you can get it?"

"Sure, there's no security whatsoever in the bookstore. He's going to be gone this weekend to a book convention in Whitefish, so I'll be able to grab it over the weekend."

"That would be wonderful. As soon as you get it, call me. Once we receive it, we'll have a lot of work to do. The map that will have a major impact on Flathead County."

"Boss, you've never mentioned the importance of this book."

"It's not the book but clues in the book that will help us keep things buried the way they should be. If someone figures it out before we do, well, let's just say there will be major problems. Make sure you get that book."

"I'm on it, Boss. It's in my hands as we speak."

"It had better be. You know what happened to the last guy who failed."

"Yeah, they found him in pieces. I sure don't want that to happen to me."

"Me either. These people don't tolerate failure."

Chapter 11

After everyone left the bookstore, Chase had gone back upstairs to check out a couple of items. He came back down to see a guy searching for something. "Can I help you?"

The guy peered up at Chase. He was the same guy that had been in the bookstore a day earlier. The guy turned and darted out the door.

Chase raced to follow him. His chest was pounding after ten minutes of tailing the fleeing man when a car pulled up. The guy opened the door, jumped in, and the car sped away. Chase was close enough to catch a glimpse of the car license plate. Once the car was out of sight, he called the Mountain Ridge Sheriff's Department.

Twenty minutes later, Detective Hall showed up at the bookstore. Chase had been sitting out front knowing better than to contaminate evidence. He slid up the wall when the detective, Kirby Hall, walked up followed by two police officers.

"Chase Connor, tell me what happened."

Chase eyed him. "Detective, a man was searching

for something in the bookstore, then ran out of the store. Don't know if he stole anything. I chased him, then lost him when he jumped into a car that pulled up. I did get his license plate number."

"Can you give it to one of the officers?" Kirby turned to the other officer. "Let's do a thorough job to see if we can find anything that would give us an idea of what this guy was searching for."

Thirty minutes later the three walked back out of the bookstore. Detective Hall asked, "We found a couple of items that we need to check. Do you know what they could be looking for?"

"I'm not sure until I check to see what's missing."

Kirby nodded to the police officer. "Go with him."

Chase grinned. "Still don't trust me."

He grinned back. "Just doing my job."

~

Sophia pulled open the door to the bar and grill to join Kirby for breakfast the next morning. He was on his cell phone when she walked in. "Already at work?" she said, smiling and sitting down across from him.

"Yeah, there was an incident at the bookstore last night involving Chase Connor."

Her eyebrows furrowed. "Is he okay?"

"He's okay. Whatever the thief was searching for, it doesn't seem like he found it, at least according to Mr. Connor."

"Are you saying Chase may be holding back information?"

Kirby's eyes widened. Sophia grimaced. "He would," she said.

"How well do you know him?"

Sophia shrugged. "I don't know him well, but my

gut reaction is, although he may have withheld information, it isn't anything illegal or harmful. He's an attorney so he knows his rights."

"That's true. Enough about him. Let's eat."

The two ordered pancakes and sausage, along with orange juice. "I'm glad you were able to join me today," Kirby said. "I have one piece of news for you, then we'll talk about anything else."

She sipped on her water. "Does it have to do with Franklin?"

"It does. Do you not want to talk about it?"

She sighed. "What happened?"

Kirby leaned forward. "The sheriff's department has called his death an accident from the car, so the case is closed."

"You don't believe that, do you?"

"Nope, but it's over, so there's nothing I can do about it. They did find the guy who hit the man and drove away. He's being charged with vehicular manslaughter."

"Could you tell me who it is?"

Kirby ran his finger through his hair. "Malcolm Smart. He's pleaded guilty to the hit-and-run accident, so he'll be sentenced in a couple of weeks."

"I know Malcolm. He does drink a lot, so it doesn't surprise me he would have hit him accidentally. He's a nice guy, but he just has a drinking problem."

Kirby sighed. "I run across them all the time, and it's so sad. Changing subjects, I heard there is a Halloween party coming up. How would you like to be my date?"

She smiled. "I'd love to. You realize we'd have to dress up in a costume, preferably matching costumes picked by the lady."

"Then I'm in your hands." He looked at his watch. "I should get to work. Are we on for tonight?" Her eyes told him she was confused. "I'm sorry. I thought I had mentioned I'd like to take you to dinner."

She batted her eyes. "If we continue this, I may start to like you a bit."

"That's my intention."

The next night Sophia and Kirby stood amidst costumed guests at the Halloween party. She was Cleopatra. He was Marc Antony. They stood drinking a beer when Willis and Allison joined them. Kirby peered at the two. "Hansel and Gretel?"

"Right on the first guess," Willis said. "What do you think?"

Sophia covered her mouth to keep from laughing. "It's exactly you, Willis. Have you seen Mom and Dad?"

"They're here somewhere dressed as a king and queen, which doesn't surprise anyone."

Kirby joined in, "Let's find a place to sit and enjoy the music."

Sophia noticed a booth over to the left of the dance floor and they headed in that direction. Sophia sat down, slid over, with Kirby sitting next to her. Allison sat across from her, with Willis sliding in next to her. The server came over with another round of beers.

"What's new in the law enforcement world?" Allison asked.

Kirby rolled his eyes. "You know I can't talk about cases we're working on. I will tell you that there is something mysterious going on at the downtown bookstore, and it's started since Connor took over."

Willis's eyes lit up. "Chase Connor? Having Chase Connor in Mountain Ridge is news in itself. I'm surprised the media hasn't gobbled it up."

Allison turned to her boyfriend. "What's so exciting about Chase?"

Willis eyed her. "Come on, he's a multi-billionaire."

"And he works at a bookstore?" Allison asked. "Is he nuts?"

Sophia jumped in. "He wants to get away from it all. I know that feeling of wanting to do that."

"Has it worked for you?" Allison asked.

She nodded as she sipped her beer. "I'm getting there, but it's taking time, but then again I'm in no hurry."

Willis directed the conversation back to Chase Connor. "What's happening at the bookstore?"

Kirby sighed. "I'm not really sure, but someone is after something in that bookstore. Chase claims he's not sure what's happening, but knowing him, he knows exactly what's happening."

Allison interrupted. "Did you know him in California?"

"I did. We had a couple of altercations, or I should say with his family. I lost both times because they are wonderful attorneys. The thing is Chase can be so much better than any of them, but he chooses to run a bookstore, which I can't figure out other than what Sophia said—he wants to find a new life."

They peered up at a doctor and a nurse who sidled up to their table. They all laughed.

"What?" Meredith grinned.

Sophia slid over so her sister could join them.

"You're very original."

Meredith blushed. "Nick always wanted to know what it was like to be a doctor, so I figured we could do it tonight, and maybe I could help him later."

They all laughed at Nick who blushed and quickly changed the subject. "I'm sorry about your manager."

"Thanks," Sophia said. "Kirby told me today it was an accident, so it's over with now, and that I'm glad about. Now I can hopefully get my life back together." Sophia tapped Kirby's hand. "Let's dance."

The group stayed there for another hour when Kirby and Sophia finally decided to call it for a night.

As Kirby opened the car door for her, he said, "How about stopping over at my apartment tonight for a nightcap?"

Sophia thought for a moment. "Why not?" She'd had a bit too much to drink and was feeling like she wanted some company this evening.

The two drove to his place, parked, and took the elevator to his apartment. He unlocked the door and stepped aside so she could enter first.

From the moment she stepped into his apartment, her eyes took in the whole place. It was small but comfortable. She adored the different photos on the walls of the Montana scenery. "Not bad."

"I'm glad you like it. I was afraid it wouldn't be good enough."

She took his hand. "It's fine. Let's sit down on the couch and talk."

The two chatted for the next hour, enjoying another couple of drinks. It was around eleven-thirty when Kirby reached over to kiss her. She responded by wrapping her arm around his head.

He stopped for a moment, moving his head back to face her. "Should we take this to the bedroom?"

She nodded. He took her hand and led her to the bedroom. They slipped out of their clothes, climbing into the bed. The next morning Sophia slipped into her clothes, and went out to make some coffee. Sophia thought about what had happened the night before. It was okay but nothing that made her feel warm all over. She held her cup feeling the cup warm her hands. If she hadn't had so much to drink, would she have crawled into bed with Kirby?

Her thoughts then focused on Chase. Would she have to have some drinks to want to sleep with him? She shivered knowing she wouldn't need them. Why did she keep having Chase in her thoughts? He had told her he didn't want her.

"There you are."

Her head turned to Kirby's voice. She smiled. "I made us some coffee."

Over the next couple of weeks, Sophia and Kirby spent time together getting to know each other. Sophia could sense he had feelings for her, but she didn't feel the same way. They had spent a couple of nights together which she was hoping would be better, but she didn't feel it. Chase interrupted her thoughts every day. How was the bookstore doing? Was he okay? Was he happy? She hadn't talked to him in two weeks.

Today Sophia decided to stop by the bookstore at closing. It was a few minutes before seven when she stopped by the door and saw in the window a gal with her arms wrapped around Chase's neck kissing him. Sophia suddenly felt weak, turned around, and hurried away.

Chapter 12

"Kady, how have you been?" Chase asked.

She dropped her arms. "I'm attending classes in Boulder and am home for the holiday break. Dad said you were here, so I had to stop by." She showed him her hand. "I'm engaged to be married."

"Congratulations."

"I grew tired of waiting for you." They both laughed. "I should get back to the house. Mom and Dad are having a social gathering to welcome me home and introduce my fiancé." She hugged him one more time. "It was great to see you. And again, thank you for what you did for me."

Chase watched her hurry out the door. The last time he had seen her was when she was seventeen. He'd saved her from a drunk college student who had sex on his mind. It was good to see Kady had grown into a beautiful gal.

Chase was almost finished with the daily business, and he'd had another good day. He was at the point where he would need to hire someone full-time. The two high school students were a tremendous help, but they could only work certain hours after school and on Saturday.

This Saturday was a big day downtown with an event called Cold Days taking place Friday and Saturday. Since November it had started to get cold around the area, so the townspeople celebrated the change of temperature with a fun event over the weekend before Thanksgiving.

The weekend started on Friday night with the actual Cold Dance itself, in which several bands performed in an area outside of the community center. At times the weather became brutally cold, but Chase was told hearty Montanans braved the cold for fun. At least he didn't have to leave the store to get a front row glimpse of the activities, since the event was right across the street from the bookstore.

The next day there were all kinds of activities that included a snowman contest, ice skating, cross-country skiing through town, plenty of warm drinks and goodies, concluding with a party at the Shepherd house that everyone was invited to.

Chase had decided to keep the bookstore open until nine on Friday night and seven on Saturday night in order to drum up more business. He was planning for the book conference in Whitefish the first weekend in December, which had been postponed because of issues dealing with the community center in Whitefish.

Chase's attention turned to Sophia. He hadn't seen her in a couple of weeks and wondered how she was doing. He should call her to see what she was up to, but then he decided against it since she was dating Kirby Hall. It was better that way.

His thoughts traveled to the book and map for

which he knew someone was searching. He had it hidden in a place no one would ever find, an old safe that was buried behind the wall upstairs. Even if the safe was found, it would be difficult to get into it because Chase had set two different codes. What did they want from it?

He had contacted a professor at the University of Montana who would meet him at the conference the weekend after Thanksgiving. Chase had volunteered to help with the Thanksgiving meal at the community center that day.

He had finished everything up in the bookstore, so he placed the money into the money bag, turned the lights off, locked the door, and walked toward the money drop at the bank. Once he completed that task, he decided to head down to the bar and grill to grab a drink. Thursday nights were usually the slowest of the week, probably because everyone was getting ready for the weekend.

It was busier than normal. He found a spot along the bar and waited for the bartender to serve him.

"Welcome," he said. "Chase Connor, correct?"

Chase eyed him. "Yes, how would you know that?"

He laughed. "Everyone knows who you are. A young lady asked me yesterday how to get a hold of you. I told her I had no clue. At my response she guzzled her drink, smiled, and left. Is that what your life is like?"

Chase laughed. "At times it can be, but I'll probably not be as popular once everyone finds out I'm broke."

"A multi-billionaire broke? How is that possible?"

"Simple, I chose to give my money to my brothers and sisters. Everyone says I'm nuts."

The guy laughed. "I wouldn't disagree." The bartender grabbed a glass to clean and pointed. "Now that gal over there has every guy chasing after her. but she's with the detective. How long that will last is anyone's guess."

"Why?" Chase asked.

The bartender picked up another glass, then turned when a couple of guys came to the bar for drinks. "Hold that thought." Five minutes later, he returned. "Sophia Shepherd dated a few guys in high school and the older dude who was her manager, but no one has ever gotten close to putting a ring on her finger. Everyone is trying to figure out who the lucky guy will be."

"And the detective?"

The bartender rubbed his beard. "It's fifty-fifty on that one. Her father is big into law enforcement, so he would be happy with that arrangement. However, Sophia is a peculiar gal whom no one can understand. She has lots of money but doesn't broadcast it like her brother does. She's kind of like you. The difference is she hasn't given her money to others."

He finished another glass. "Maybe you should see how you fare with the gal?"

Chase laughed. "Way out of my league. Too beautiful, classy, and a model to top it off."

"Yeah, she was a damn good model. I don't know why she quit. Who knows about a Shepherd? By the way, my name is Jacob Myer."

Chase stuck out his hand and grinned. "Nice to meet you."

"I should get back to work. Don't forget the Cold

Dance tomorrow night. There will be a lot of things happening that you won't believe."

"I heard about it." Chase set his drink down, started to walk out, but stopped when he saw Sophia looking his way. He nodded, and she turned away. Jacob Myer was wrong about the two of them hooking up from the glare Kirby had just given him. What did he do wrong now?

Chapter 13

Sophia had sucked down another beer. Seeing Chase with that gal around his neck had bothered her, but she didn't know why other than she wanted him to kiss her, not some other gal. She turned when Kirby placed his arms around her shoulders. "Are you ready to go home?"

She turned around. "Not tonight. I'm going home to my own bed."

"Is everything okay?"

She nodded. "I just need to sleep alone tonight." She grabbed her jacket, hurried out the door, then headed toward her destination—the hotel. Sophia had heard that Chase had moved back into the hotel two days ago, now that the Boyd gal was back for the holidays. She waited for the slow-moving doors to open in the hotel then walked in.

"Sophia Shepherd, what brings you to our lovely hotel?"

She smiled. "Anthony, you're still working here? I thought you'd be off to see the world by now."

He grimaced. "Things didn't seem to work out, but

I'm still trying. What can I do for you?"

"I'm searching for my boyfriend, but he forgot to let me know what room he was in. He arrived not too long ago."

Anthony smiled. "I remember him. You picked a winner since he's a nice guy."

"That would be him."

Sophia took the elevator to the third floor, stepped off, looked at the room number signs on the wall, and headed in that direction. She stood in front of Room 313 and knocked on the door.

Chase opened the door. "Sophia, what are you doing here?"

She wrapped her arms around his neck, kicked the door closed behind her, and pushed him toward the bed where he fell backwards. She climbed on top, kissing him, then reached for his belt buckle.

"Hold it, this isn't going to happen." He lifted her off of him, rolling her onto the bed. "What are you doing?"

She sat up. "What does it look like I'm doing? I want to crawl into bed with you."

He sighed and pulled her toward him. "A couple of reasons why that won't work. First, you're dating another guy, and I'd sure hate to find out my girlfriend was in bed with another guy."

She reached to kiss him. "He doesn't have to know. I'll never tell him."

He put his arms up to hold her shoulders. "Second, you're drunk, and I'll never take advantage of a gal who's had too much to drink."

She eyed him. "Is it because I'm not young enough? I'm not seventeen?"

He sighed. "This is not happening."

She fell back on the bed and was out. He covered her up. "Sophia, this is not you. What's going on?" Once he knew she was sleeping soundly, he crawled over to the chair and was sacked out almost immediately.

The morning light filtered into the room. His eyes popped open when he felt her eyes boring into him.

"Why won't you kiss me like you did that gal at the bookstore the other night?"

"Is that what this is all about? You saw me kissing another girl? Oh, that was Dr. Boyd's daughter, and I've known her since she was twelve. We've become good friends over the years. She just came in to give me a hug."

"How was I supposed to know that? You're supposed to be kissing me, not every gal that shows up in your bookstore. You've ignored me the past few weeks."

"Whoa, ignored you? You're with Detective Kirby Hall, and from what I understand, you two are pretty close."

"That's because you decided you wanted to spend time reading books instead of being with me."

Chase stood up. "Put your clothes on, and I'll take you home."

She stood up naked except for her panties. "I'm not drunk now, and you've seen everything there is to see on me. All you have to do is pull down my panties, and that'll be it. My upper part might not be like most other gals, but I'm happy with them."

Chase grabbed her dress and slipped it over her. "Put your heels on. You're going home."

She did as he asked, then the two caught the elevator. They walked past the manager's desk.

"How did it go last night, Sophia?"

She frowned. "Not like I expected."

Once the two reached Sophia's house, she opened the door, turned to him, and peered into his eyes. "I made a fool of myself last night. Can we try again another night?"

"Goodbye, Sophia." Chase drove back to the bookstore, walked upstairs, and opened the safe. He carefully lifted the old book out and flipped through the pages. What was so special about this book? It featured maps of Montana, as well as historical information about various areas of the state, but there were plenty of other books like this one.

Chase thumbed through the pages, then eyed the cover. He felt along the back of the book noticing the cover was different from the inside of the back cover. It was much softer, which made him wonder. He thought about it for a moment. What if the whole inside back cover and front cover had been changed from the original because something was hidden in it?

He felt around the edge of the back cover, finally finding something. It had been glued, but part of it didn't hold. Chase continued gently pulling the back cover apart and found a map.

It could be another clue. Now he just had to put the pieces together to see what it meant. If he had that long before someone stole it.

Chapter 14

"Are you going to just stand there and daydream?" Kirby came up, standing next to her. She reached up, put her arms around him, and kissed him solidly on the lips.

At the same time, Sophia kept her eyes on Chase who had already stepped back into the bookstore. She had hoped to make him jealous. "Damn it."

"What?" Kirby asked.

"Nothing, I just tripped on my foot. Should we go dancing?" Sophia was drinking way more than she needed to that night. She took Kirby's hand. "We really need to head to your apartment."

"Are you okay?" he asked. She kissed him. "Oh, I get it."

Once they finished, Kirby rolled over and fell fast asleep. Sophia wiped the tears off her cheeks. She was losing control of everything—popping diet pills, drinking, and jumping into bed with men. If she continued down this path, she could do some real damage, both physical and moral. She finally fell asleep.

The next morning, she woke up early, slipped into her clothes, then sat on the side of the bed staring at Kirby. Where was this relationship going? Was he the reason she was doing these things? It was always easy to blame someone else when one's life was out of control. It started unraveling when she spent the night with Chase. She wished he had done so much more than just hold her, but she could understand his reasoning that she had a boyfriend.

"How can you already be daydreaming this early in the morning?"

She smiled. "A lot is going on today. Tonight, my parents have their annual event which will be a pain."

"You'll get through it," Kirby said, reaching over to kiss her.

"You won't be there?"

"Yeah, but I'll be working, so I'll be able to keep my eye on you."

Her head shot up. "What did you say?"

He grinned. "I'll be able to watch over you while I'm watching over the whole event."

She climbed off the bed. "I should get going."

He put his arm around her. "I'll see you afterward for a dance and more."

She peered at him. "Maybe." She scurried out of the apartment then stopped to take a breath. Her heart was beating faster than normal. Taking measured breaths, she was able to control it. What was happening to her?

A familiar voice caught her attention. Sophia turned to Allison, who was hurrying over with Willis. "Did you bring the stuff I asked for?" Sophia asked.

"I got it. Here you go. Willis is here to cheer us

on."

They walked up to the registration tent. Once that was completed, Allison asked, "Are you ready for the snowman sculpting contest? I'm ready. I have a couple of ideas."

"Let's hear them." Sophia said.

"We could give him some kind of different hairstyle like a mohawk or even braids. I have hairstyling stuff in that bag."

Willis laughed. "I like that idea."

"I do too," Sophia said. "I also brought some items we could use to do that. You could also have our snowman reading a book, which would be unique."

"Cool idea. When do we start?" Allison asked.

"Right now. We have thirty minutes to sculpt our masterpiece before they judge them, with the winners being announced at noon," Sophia said.

"What do we get this year?"

Willis grinned. "Six months of ice-skating rink passes and get this—a photo by your snowman that will be displayed on the Cold Dance Wall of Fame."

Sophia packed a snowball, and the two rolled it on the ground, which drew a laugh from the group as the two fell down several times, but they finally finished the base then took a break.

Allison grinned. "That is a lot of work."

"And we've just started," Sophia laughed. She peered across the street to see Chase watching the activities.

"Let's go," Allison said.

Fifteen minutes later the duo had the snowman how they wanted it. Allison reached into the bag, brought out some buttons, and Sophia placed two for the eyes and buttons for the coat. Sophia found some string and fastened them on the head to make it look like headphones, which drew a laugh from those in the audience.

Finally, Allison had placed stringy red yarn on its head. Allison looked at her and grinned.

"What?"

"Mohawk or long hair?"

"Long hair, of course, since we have a snowman with glasses reading a book," Sophia quipped.

~

The judges ended up evaluating seven snowmen, including one by three six-year-old girls, for whom everyone had cheered throughout the event. It boiled down to two snowmen, and the judges couldn't decide between them.

After another ten minutes of deliberation, they made their decision. Everyone gathered around as one of the judges spoke up. "This has been an entertaining snowman event, that's for sure. We've had a snowman who reads books, a country singer, and even a snowman monkey, which was quite clever."

He sipped on apple cider. "It was a tough decision, but we've decided to go with the snowman monkey."

The three little girls jumped up and down, hollering, "We won. We won."

"You did," the judge said. The judges wrapped medals around the three girls' necks and then took photos of them for the Wall of Fame. One of the judges strode to the podium. "In addition, here are your tickets for six months of free ice skating in the winter months and roller skating in the warmer months. Congratulations to all of the contestants for a wonderful snowman event."

A lady hurried over and whispered to the judge. He nodded and spoke in the mic. "One other thing, this year the local churches have banded together to put together the first Cold Dance lunch. It's ready, so enjoy."

~

Chase enjoyed watching the activities happening on the main street. The two high school students who had been working told him they needed to leave because they were participating in different events. He stepped back into the bookstore. There were several people browsing around for books.

An older lady with curly gray hair touched his arm. "I'm looking for a historical book with maps."

"Do you know the title of the book?"

She thought for a moment. "It has to do with Montana myths and historical events, but I can't remember the title."

Chase led her to the history section. "Here is the shelves with all the historical books. If you knew the name of it, then I could help you more."

"Everyone has been searching for this book, but no one has been able to find it. However, a man said he thought he had seen it here."

"How about the cover or anything about the book?"

She thought for a moment. "Large book with a normal hard cover but a softer type of cover inside."

"That's unusual, unless somebody changed the cover."

She shrugged. "I wouldn't know, but I'll look through here to see what I can find."

"Good luck. If you need anything let me know." He started to leave but stopped when she kept talking.

"I shall. You're much nicer than the former owner. He could be grumpy."

He smiled. "Thank you for the compliment."

"Now if I could just find that blasted book, I'd be ecstatic."

Throughout the rest of the day the bookstore stayed busy, his busiest day since he'd opened the business two months ago. It was past nine when he locked the bookstores and headed toward the Shepherds.

Chapter 15

Sophia came out of the Shepherds 'bathroom after taking one of her pills. She stopped when she saw Chase. "You shouldn't be here, especially when I'm on a date with Kirby."

"You said this was the place to be tonight. You're looking pretty."

She blushed. "Why are you always so nice to me?"

He eyed her. "No matter how you feel, you're a nice gal."

Sophia took a deep breath, knowing that she wanted him to take her into his arms and never let her go. But this was real life. "Thanks. I should get back to my date." She grabbed another drink, found Kirby and the others, and joined them.

"There you are," Allison said.

"I just needed to use the ladies' room, but I'm ready to party all night."

"That's what we're talking about," Allison said.

Over the next hour, the group continued drinking, laughing, and enjoying their time together. At times, Sophia kept her eyes out for Chase, but she didn't see him. Kirby and Sophia stepped out onto the floor to dance. She wrapped her arms around her neck and peered into his eyes. "I'm thinking tonight we could spend the whole night in bed. What do you think?"

He eyed her. "That's not like you."

She kissed him again. "We're getting to know each other better. Once that happens, I'll feel better about things. What about it?" Just then, the room spun, and Sophia fell to the floor and started convulsing. She couldn't control herself, then the world went black.

~*

Kirby dropped down beside her. "Hang in there." He peered up as Chase slid down by him and said, "I called for an ambulance. Since the seizures have stopped, I'll work on the chest while you give her mouth-to-mouth."

The two worked together, and Chase finally found a pulse. "Don't you dare die now," He whispered to her. A moment later, she sputtered. She peered into his eyes, and then hers closed.

They tried once more to revive her but couldn't. The EMTs arrived and took over. "She still has a faint breath." He stuck a defibrillator on her and finally got her back. They lifted her gently onto the stretcher, and they moved her to the ambulance which took minutes later.

~*

Sophia stared around at the white walls. Where was she? What had happened? She wasn't sure what was happening, although she knew it wasn't good.

Several moments later she noticed what looked like her mother and father standing in the room with Willis and Allison. Once everyone had left, she tried to fall asleep but noticed Meredith standing over her. She tried to say hi, but her lips were so dry. Her eyes were fading, but she heard Meredith say, "You're going to make it."

~

Meredith finished her rounds and headed back to the nurse's station seeing Chase sitting on a bench outside of Sophia's room. She sat down next to him. "What happened to Kirby?"

"He went to grab some coffee for the two of us."

"She's going to be just fine although the pills didn't help any."

"I'm just glad she's going to be okay."

"You care a lot about her, don't you?"

Chase shook his head. "She's better off with the detective. All I'd cause are problems, and she's had plenty of those in the past few years."

Meredith took a deep breath. "How can you believe something like that?"

"I'm Chase Connor. That's enough."

Meredith shrugged. "Are you somebody special?"

Chase laughed. "Everyone believes that, but I just happen to be the son of a multi-billionaire meaning everyone knows who I am. You're the first person who doesn't."

She grinned. "Unless the patient tells me about it, I have no clue, but I will tell you that what happened to Sophia isn't directly your fault. It's her issue, so quit feeling sorry for yourself. I'm sure you have your own issues to deal with."

"You'd be right. I purchased a bookstore, and I'm also thinking about combining it with an antique store. How crazy is that?"

"It's not crazy. The two would mix well together. I'd be interested to see how it turns out if you should purchase the other business." She stood up. "Right now, I have to get back to work. Don't beat yourself up so badly over my sister's issues. She'll be fine."

~

The next morning Nathan and Ophelia Shepherd hurried into the hospital. As they walked toward Sophia's room, Ophelia noticed Chase and Kirby sitting on chairs in the hallway. They both seemed half asleep. Meredith strode toward them.

"Were they here all night?" she asked Meredith.

She nodded. "They paced the halls, stopped at the doorway to check on her, and even stepped in to talk to her. She was out of it, but Chase said something to her that made her perk up. What he said, I don't know."

"How is she doing?" Nathan asked.

"Much better. It may be awhile before she's better, and she'll have a tough road ahead of her. I'll let the doctor explain to you. He should be making his rounds any moment now."

The Shepherds sat down on chairs inside the room watching their daughter breathing. Ophelia wiped a tear off her cheek. "What happened to her?"

"I'm not sure, honey. We'll find out soon."

They peered up when the doctor walked in. They jumped off their chairs. "What can you tell us?" Nathan asked.

"It's not good, but she'll survive…at least this time."

Nathan and Ophelia were confused. "Tell us what's happened to her?" her mother said.

The doctor took a deep breath. "Let's step outside

to talk." Once they were outside, the doctor turned to them. "She mixed alcohol with amphetamines last night. How long has she been taking diet pills?"

They both shrugged.

"It's a weight loss product, but it's also an upper that's highly addictive. The problem is when mixed with alcohol, it makes a person feel more depressed and anxious. It also increases the risk of high blood pressure, elevated heart rate, and chest pain, even going as far as heart failure."

"Oh my gosh," Ophelia said, covering her mouth. "Every model takes them, but she's left that life."

The doctor continued. "It appears she's been doing it secretly for many months. Until we check her heart, I'm not sure what kind of impact it has had on her. The next few days will be critical for your daughter. It would be good once she leaves here to get her into an environment she feels comfortable in. You might want to consider rehab."

Once the doctor left, the Shepherds held each other. "What has she done?" Ophelia asked.

"I don't know, but she'll pull through. The question is what type of environment would be good for her. Certainly not drug rehab."

She turned back to what was happening in the room. Sophia opened her eyes. "I'm sorry, Mom, Dad, for putting you through this."

"You scared us to death," Nathan said. "What were you thinking?"

Ophelia touched his hand. "Not now, Nathan. She's been through enough."

Sophia peered around the room then back at his parents. "Was Kirby here?"

Meredith entered and eyed her sister. "He and Chase were both here all night, pacing back and forth outside in the hallway, checking the room every once in a while to make sure you were okay."

"I thought I heard someone standing over my bed."

Meredith nodded. "They both told you it was going to be okay because you were a strong gal who had her whole life ahead of her. It must have helped because several times you would wake up shaking and sweating, but by the time we were in the room, you had calmed down."

Sophia nodded. "I heard someone's voice, but I wasn't sure who it was."

Meredith peered at her. "They spoke softly to you. Their voices soothed you, because you went right back to sleep. Their voices helped more than any of our drugs did." Meredith turned to her parents. "Mom, Dad, she's going to be okay, but she does need her rest right now."

"We understand," Ophelia said.

Once Meredith left, Ophelia turned to her daughter. "What is it with you and the young Connor boy?"

"I don't know, Mom, he makes me so blasted mad at times, but I do care about him."

"Even more than the police detective?" Nathan asked.

"Yes, but it wouldn't matter anyway because Chase told me to try to build a relationship with Kirby, which I'm trying to do, but every time I believe things are going smoothly, something about Chase pops up in my mind, somebody talks about the bookstore, or I see him kiss another gal."

Ophelia's eyes widened. "What were you doing,

spying on him?"

Sophia's eyes opened. "No, Mom, I hadn't seen him for a couple of weeks, so I went to the bookstore, saw him in the window with this girl's arms around his neck, planting a solid kiss on him. Where's the justice in that?"

"You're feeling better," Ophelia said. "We'll let you get some sleep."

The two strolled out of the room. "What was that all about?"

Ophelia took her husband's hand. "Dear, our daughter is in love."

"With Chase Connor?"

"No, I think two guys."

He stopped and stared at her. "They're the ones who are killing her?"

"Where would you get an idea like that? My thought is she's been taking those pills for a long time because of the modeling, kept them around, but when she saw the gal kissing Chase, it scared her, and that was how she reacted. She also feels strongly about Kirby."

"I'll break both their necks."

Ophelia glared at him. "You'll do no such thing. Didn't you hear Meredith say how his voice helped her through? Chase loves her also, but he won't do anything because she's with another guy."

"What are we going to do?" Nathan asked.

"I don't know, but I'm going to have a talk with Chase."

Ophelia drove to the bookstore that afternoon. He was busy with a customer when she walked in.

"Mrs. Shepherd, I can't believe you're searching

for a book with a library like yours."

She grinned. "As you well know, even the rich can read."

"I've heard that. What can I do for you?"

She took off her gloves. "Do you have time to talk?"

He nodded. "Would you like a cup of coffee?"

"That would be great."

Chase came back a few minutes later carrying coffee mugs. "I brought you some packets of cream and sugar also."

"Thank you."

Chase pulled a chair out for her.

"My daughter said you had manners. Thank you."

He sat down across from her. "How is Sophia?"

"She's doing well thanks to you and your soft voice."

He sighed. "I did what I could to help her. I kept telling her she's strong, and she'll make it through."

She sipped on her coffee. "Did you actually say, 'why are you breaking my heart?' or something like that? Sophia wasn't sure what you had said, but she told me those were the words that she thought she heard."

Chase grimaced. "I never meant for that to come out. I'm sorry she heard that. That's not why you're here. What is on your mind?"

Ophelia laughed. "Chase Connor, just like his father, right to the point."

"I don't know if that's good or bad, but that's what happens."

She sipped on her coffee. "You're right. I'm here asking you for your help."

Chase waited.

"The doctor said she needs a relaxing atmosphere, and it seems that she's talked about working with books, so I was wondering if you would be able to hire her here."

Chase frowned. "Since it's not her decision to work here, I won't help her. Now if she comes and asks, it'll be different, but I had parents who tried to decide who I should be with, what I should do, and I'd never do that to Sophia."

She grinned. "You sure you're a Connor?"

Chase laughed. "Unfortunately, that's what I've been told. I care about your daughter, but she's dating another guy, and there are so many things she doesn't know about me."

"Then tell her."

Chase sighed. "Once she finds out who I was, it'll never be the same. She cares about Kirby."

She turned to Chase. "Would you like to join us for Thanksgiving Dinner?"

"If you're asking me for yourself not for your daughter, then yes."

Ophelia smiled once more. "Of course, it's for me."

Just as she was prepared to walk out the door, Chase's voice stopped her. "You should smile more. Your smile is as beautiful as Sophia's."

"Maybe you should tell her that."

Chapter 16

Sophia was eating her Jello when Willis and Allison joined her. "You must be feeling better if you're eating hospital food," Allison grinned.

"It's actually good. This is the third helping I've had this afternoon. What brings you two here?"

Willis hugged his sister. "Wanted to make sure you were okay. What were you thinking?"

Allison nudged her boyfriend. "Sophia doesn't need to hear your nonsense. She's trying to get better, and I'm sure she feels horrible about what happened."

Sophia finished eating her Jello.

Her brother stared at her. "Aren't you even going to talk about it?"

"Nope."

"That's just it—nope?" Willis said. "You realize what it's done to our family?"

Allison nudged Willis once more. "Enough. Let her regain her strength before you delve into that."

"That makes sense," Willis said, turning to Sophia. "I'm sorry about the way I acted."

Sophia eyed her brother. "I'm not going to get into

it with you right now, but I know you believe I've disrespected the family, and that's something I'm going to have to deal with by myself."

Later that day, she had just woken up from a nap when Kirby stopped in. He smiled at her. "How are you feeling?"

Sophia reached out her hand, taking his. "I'm doing well. How about you?"

"Been busy. I'm sorry I haven't stopped by, but since there could be criminal charges involved, I had to stay away."

"It's safe to say that there won't be any criminal charges."

He sighed. "You're right, which is good news."

"Do you have any plans for Thanksgiving?" Sophia said, taking a sip of water from the straw.

"I don't. What did you have in mind?"

"Why don't you join me for my family's annual Thanksgiving meal. It's quite a spectacular event."

The next morning, the day before Thanksgiving, the doctor said Sophia was good to go.

Her parents were there to pick her up. "Are you ready to go home, dear?" her mother asked.

"I am, but no big parties. Do you understand, Dad?"

"Understood."

When they pulled into the driveway, Sophia stepped out of the car and looked at the house. "I never realized how large this place was, or how opulent."

Her mother put her arm around Sophia's shoulder. "It's always been that way."

Sophia peered at her mother. "I have a couple of things I need to do." She walked toward the door, stopped, and peered at her parents. "I'll be all right, but I'm going to do it myself, so please don't worry about me." When she entered the foyer, there stood several of the servants. They all hugged her and told her they were glad to see her. Sophia brushed tears away as she walked up the twenty-two stairs to the next floor. She didn't realize how time-consuming it could be.

Once she was in her bedroom, she perused the whole room—the king-sized bed, several photos of herself over the years on the wall, a large television screen hanging from another wall, and a massive window with a view of the mountains. She loved the view, but the rest made her wonder.

She walked over to close the curtains, then went into the bathroom to run some hot water in her jacuzzi hot tub. Could she survive without it? She could.

Once the tub was full, she stripped out of her clothes, climbed in, and sank down toward the bottom of the tub. It felt so good. She came back up to relax her head against the porcelain back, turning on the jets.

Sophia closed her eyes and thought about what had transpired over the last couple of years. She had enjoyed modeling at the start, but it became such a drain on her both physically and mentally, that she had to resort to pills to help her along. When she arrived in Montana in October, she had hoped to start her life all over again, but the habit had carried over.

Once finished soaking, Sophia slid into a blue knee-length dress and closed-toed heels. She walked down the stairs running into her father.

"Where are you going dressed like that?"

"I have an interview for a job. I'll let you know what happens."

Sophia drove toward the bookstore, parked the car in one of the customer spots, and walked into the building.

Chase peered up from what he was doing to see her. "You look nice," he said.

She blushed at his gaze and brushed her wind-blown hair out of her eyes. "Please, I'm here for a job interview, not to be doted over."

"I'm sorry. How did you know I was looking for help?"

She grinned. "Not much to do when you're lying in a hospital bed. I saw the ad to work at a bookstore, so I thought I'd apply."

Chase took a deep breath. "Sorry, but it would never work out between the two of us. You belong with Kirby."

She frowned. "I'm just applying for a job."

"And I'm telling you I'm not hiring you for this job. It'll cause problems between you and Kirby, and I won't let that happen."

"You seem to have everything figured out." She glared at him. "Maybe you're right. Maybe I belong with Kirby."

Chapter 17

Thanksgiving Day arrived in Mountain Ridge, Montana, and Ophelia, Sophia, and Meredith were in the kitchen cooking the turkey.

While she was stirring the mashed potatoes, Sophia stared out at the snow coming down. "I've missed these blizzards."

"How did the job interview go?" Meredith asked.

Sophia peered up at her. "How did you know about that?"

She sighed. "A newspaper left on the hospital tray with the job circled for the bookstore. It didn't take a brain surgeon to figure that one out."

Sophia frowned. "He told me no."

"What?" Ophelia raised her voice.

"Calm down, Mom," Meredith said.

"I'm calm," Ophelia said. "What happened?"

Sophia continued mashing the potatoes. "He told me he didn't want to get in between Kirby and me."

"That makes sense," Meredith said. "Besides, you are with Kirby, aren't you?"

Sophia shrugged. "I am, but I want to have

choices."

"Bad move," Meredith said.

They had finished putting together the meal and bringing it out to the table when the doorbell rang. "I'll get it," Sophia said. She hurried to the door and opened it. Her eyes widened. "Chase, what are you doing here? What did you do to your hair?"

He grinned. "I cut it because I was meeting the folks."

Her mother hurried over. "I invited him. Chase doesn't like your parents telling you how to run your life, or something like that." She turned to Chase. "Welcome, and join us."

"I'm sorry I'm late. I just finished helping with the Thanksgiving Dinner downtown. It's amazing how many people showed up." Chase followed Sophia and the others into the dining room.

Nathan jumped up and shook his hand. "Chase, how wonderful for you to join us." Chase looked stunned but shook his hand. Sophia's eyes widened at the scene also. Willis said hi.

Just then Kirby walked into the room and took a seat.

"Awkward," Meredith said quietly when she walked up to Chase.

Chase turned to her. "Not really."

Ophelia introduced her parents. Her father stood and shook his hand. Chase nodded at Ophelia's mother. Then he peered around the table. "Allison couldn't make it?"

Willis spoke up, "She spends Thanksgiving with her parents."

Once they all took seats, they passed the food

around after saying a prayer of thanks. Chase took a bite of his turkey. "This is very good."

Sophia's grandmother dabbed at her lips with her napkin. "Chase, what's a Connor Thanksgiving in California like?"

"Much the same, although there wouldn't be a blizzard happening like today."

Nathan nodded. "We're expected to get ten to twelve inches of snow with thirty-forty mile-per-hour winds. You'll get used to it."

"How's the bookstore going?" Sophia's grandfather asked.

"Surprisingly well," he said. "I'm going to a book sellers conference next weekend in Whitefish where I hope to purchase more old books, which people around here seem to enjoy."

The older man finished chewing his piece of turkey. "I don't understand how a young guy with billions of dollars would want to be a bookseller."

"Dad," Ophelia jumped in.

Chase lifted his hand. "It's okay, Mrs. Shepherd. I've wondered that myself many times while stacking books. I enjoy reading them for sure, but the biggest reason I bought the place was to prove to my family and myself that I could do something on my own. I'll fail or succeed on my own. Right now, I'm doing well."

Willis spoke for the first time. "Mr. Boer was always so grumpy and didn't have a good assortment of books, so many people stayed away."

Chase nodded. "I had heard that, but I don't believe it since I got to know him before he left. Now, I'm thinking about talking to Mr. Harper about purchasing the antique shop to combine the two."

"Interesting," Nathan said. "How are you going to pay for it since your father took away all your money?"

"Dad, knock it off. It's none of your business," Sophia said.

Chase sighed. "I have the means. Mr. Harper has a wonderful family, in particular three grandchildren who have a lot of energy."

Ophelia jumped in. "Oh, Maci's kids—or I should say—her step kids. She married a guy who had three children from his first marriage. I believe he's fifteen years older than Maci."

The grandfather spoke up. "There seems to be a lot of that going on around here."

"Now, Dad, quit being such a downer on Thanksgiving," Ophelia said.

After the meal, everyone went out to the living room to watch the football game. Sophia and Kirby disappeared upstairs.

Chase took the opportunity to get a breath of fresh air. He stepped outside. Despite the blizzard-like temperature, the snow was beautiful, the air crisp. He lingered outside until his fingers began to freeze. Why hadn't he worn his coat? He slapped his arms.

The door opened and Meredith popped out. "Here, you'll need this if you stay out here long enough." Meredith handed Chase a cup of hot chocolate. "And this." He pulled on his coat while she held his cocoa.

"Thanks," he said, wrapping both hands around the hot chocolate. "Where's Nick?"

After taking a sip of her hot cocoa, she spoke. "Let's just say Nick and my father don't get along too well. Dad doesn't like the idea that I'm the major breadwinner in the relationship, since Nick has a tough time holding down jobs."

"I'm sorry to hear that."

Meredith peered up at him. "Don't be. Nick has had a couple of bad breaks. We'll be okay. He spends the holidays with his family in Helena."

Chase blew out a breath and watched it float in the air. "You sure are a positive person."

She shrugged. "Being a nurse you have to be, since everyone I deal with has an ailment of sorts, and they need some positivity in their lives to keep going."

"I can understand that. What made you decide to become a nurse, especially with who your family is?"

She sipped her drink. "I wanted to help people and believed nursing was the quickest way to achieve that goal. I'm also working on my doctorate degree, and I'm getting closer every day to finish it. What about you? Is it true you're an attorney?"

"Yes, I am. Dr. Boyd had asked me to join his law firm out here, but I told him I wanted nothing to do with practicing anymore, which led me to the bookstore and antique shop decision."

Meredith offered a derisive grin. "I'm sure your parents are happy about your decision."

He thought about the comment. "Actually, they were okay with it, which surprised me, since my father has always wanted his children to do things his way. I'm nervous and excited at the same time about my new venture, but then again, I'll make it or fail on my own merits, not someone else's."

"I may have to stop by and check out the bookstore. I haven't been there since high school when our history teacher took us on a tour of different venues around Mountain Ridge, and the bookstore was one of them. He isn't married and lives and breathes history. The history teacher would be a good person to talk to about old things."

"I'll remember that. Perhaps you can give me his name later on."

She shivered. "Of course. I'm getting cold, so I'm going to step back inside. Don't stay out too long. I'd hate to see you in the hospital with frostbite." She grinned.

An hour later, Chase joined the others who were watching the football game. The grandparents were fast asleep, while the others' eyes were glued to the television. Meredith scooted over on the couch so Chase could sit down.

"Who's winning?" he asked.

"Cowboys," she whispered.

"Go, Rams." He smiled.

The others glared at him. "I'm sorry," he grimaced.

Meredith leaned over and whispered to him, "Go Rams."

When the game had finished, Ophelia's grandfather told Willis to go find Sophia. "It's time to play cards."

Fifteen minutes later, Sophia and Kirby walked into the kitchen where everyone was sitting around the table.

Her grandfather glanced at his watch. "Sophia, you know four-thirty is card-playing time on Thanksgiving Day. You're fifteen minutes late."

Sophia grinned. "Sorry, Grandpa. We're ready now."

As the two grabbed seats, Sophia's grandmother smiled. "Sophia, you look radiant. It must have been a wonderful nap."

Chapter 18

The next day Chase met with Mr. Harper about the antique shop. After an hour of negotiating, they finally produced a figure satisfactory for both parties.

Mr. Harper peered at Chase. "Before I make any final decisions, I'd like you to talk to my family about your plans."

"I can wait. In the meantime, are you okay with me contacting a contractor to give me some ideas on remodeling the place?"

"That's fine."

As soon as the meeting was over, Chase opened his shop and contacted Matt Leopold who said he would meet him after lunch. The time went quickly because so many customers came in to buy or browse.

At one o'clock, Chase put the closed sign on the door, and he walked over to the bar and grill for his lunch. He took a seat at the bar.

"Well, if it isn't the new owner of a bookstore and antique shop."

Chase rolled his eyes. "Jake, how did you find out so quickly?"

He smiled. "I'm the owner of a bar and grill, and everyone likes to gossip. You're purchasing those two businesses has been the talk of the town for the past twenty-four hours. How are things going?"

"Just getting started with the remodeling phase. I'll talk to all of the employees to see where they stand, but I do hope they decide to stay with me, since that would make the transition much easier. Now I'll just have to find some managers."

"Maci Harper would be a wonderful hire. She knows all kinds of stuff about the antique business, since she's helped her father over the past few years. The problem is her husband. In fact, there they are right now."

Chase turned to Maci, a balding guy, and three children. She peered his way and waved at him. Chase gave her a two-finger salute then turned back to Jacob. "What is it about young gals marrying older men in Montana?"

Jacob grinned. "There just aren't enough younger guys to go around for the gals in the state. Really, I can't explain the reasoning behind it, but those two certainly will never make it together. They're two very different people."

Chase studied Jacob. "You continue to surprise me. Not only are you a bartender, but you're also a marriage counselor. What else can you do?"

"I'm a pretty good matchmaker. Well, I should get going." The bartender went back to washing glasses.

Chase took a bite of his sandwich then saw Meredith and her boyfriend, Nick, walking in together. They both nodded his way. He did the same.

Jacob joined Chase and brought him another beer.

"Now Meredith and Nick are a cute couple, but I don't know how long Nick will stay here with her."

"What does that mean?"

Jacob washed one of his glasses. "His parents live in Salt Lake City; they want him to come home to help with the family business. He's contemplating doing it."

"What is the family business?"

"Construction. The father is getting near retirement, and he wants Nick to take the business over, since he's the only child in the family. Meredith is not saying no, but they're holding back until she finds a nurse's job in Salt Lake City."

"It shouldn't be that hard," Chase said. "Health care professionals are needed everywhere."

"True," Jacob said, placing the glass on the counter with the others. "She's one gal I can't just figure out. Meredith loves her job, but I'm not sure if she loves Nick as much, but then again, it's none of my business."

"That it isn't. I should get going." He stood and threw some bills on the bar.

Jacob picked up his plate, then rang up the bill. "Don't forget to come in tonight. The local band will be performing right here, and we'll be offering half-price drinks."

"How do you stay in business with half-price drinks?"

Jacob smiled. "Montanans love their liquor."

Chase hurried over to the antique shop where Mr. Harper was waiting for him. "Is it a done deal?"

He shook his hand and nodded. "I have a few things to go over with you, then the business is all yours." Mr. Harper handed him the signed legal documents, then he spent the next few hours teaching him the business. He finished by handing him some documents for items on order. "Also, you have to drive to Helena soon to pick up a chest that was given to us by an antique collector in the city."

"Why would he give you the chest?" Chase asked.

Mr. Harper shrugged. "He said he'd heard we run a respectable business, and he wanted it out of his house. We don't ask questions; we just move the items that people provide us."

After a couple more items, Mr. Harper handed Chase the keys. "Good luck. The wife and I are taking our first trip in a couple of years. If you need any help, contact Maci or Meredith. Either one will help out."

Five minutes after Mr. Harper left the antique shop, Mr. Leopold walked in with a smile. "You're going to keep me busy, Chase."

"I plan on it, at least for the time being. Do you want to look around here and then head back to the bookstore for a cup of coffee?"

"Sounds like a plan." The two checked out the antique shop, which was just a bit larger than the bookstore. The upstairs was the same size. "What do you plan on doing upstairs?" Mr. Leopold said.

"I'm not really sure. Of course, we could turn it into an apartment, but I'm willing to listen to any other ideas."

Mr. Leopold stood in the doorway searching the area. "Another idea would be to turn this area into a showroom, or it could become another business. That's something you'll have to think about—what kind of business you would want."

Chase sighed. "Two businesses is enough at this

point. A showroom may be an idea."

"Where do you plan on living?"

Chase offered a grin. "I've found a cabin I'm interested in near Smith Lake; that is, if I can afford it. If not, I'll sleep in one of these apartments."

Mr. Leopold placed his hand in his pocket. "You'll have to decide on what direction you wish to go with all of this."

Chase was quiet for a moment. "Let's turn this into a showroom and use the bedrooms as a storage area."

The man took a few more notes, then snapped a few pictures of the room with his phone. "I'll put an estimate together, and we'll get started."

After Mr. Leopold left, Chase spent the day inventorying what he had in the antique store while one of the high school students handled the bookstore until it closed at seven.

It was past five when the door opened. Chase turned to see Meredith walk in.

"I stopped by to see how things are going."

He shrugged. "Slow at the moment."

Meredith took off her coat. "Let me give you a hand."

"You're not working tonight?"

"Not tonight. What do you need me to do?"

He handed her a clipboard. "If you can help me with the inventory list, I'd appreciate it."

"Consider it done."

Over the next two hours, the two added to the list. "I thought Mr. Harper would have an inventory list of his own," Meredith said.

Chase grinned. "He was ready to hightail it out of here."

Meredith laughed. "The man's been like that for the past two years." She stopped for a moment and stared at Chase. "You realize antique stores don't make a lot of money."

"Maybe I can change that."

"Maybe."

Meredith looked up at the clock. "I should be going. I'm supposed to meet Nick at the bar and grill at eight for our romantic night together."

Chase eyed her. "Romantic night?"

Meredith smiled. "Nick always tries to make our date nights romantic. Just the fact that we're together—I'm okay with that. What about you?"

Chase shook his head. "I have to drive to Whitefish tomorrow for a book conference, so I'm going to spend some more time here."

She posted her hands on her hips. "Chase, don't bury your life in books and antiques, or you'll burn out awfully quick."

He opened the door for her and told her to have fun with her boyfriend.

Chase spent another couple of hours working on the inventory, then glanced up at the clock, seeing it was nine. He shook his head. Meredith was right. He should relax. Around nine-thirty he arrived at the bar and grill. The place was crowded with loud music and people dancing.

Chase ambled over to the bar. "Busy night."

Jacob nodded. "Friday nights are always busy, especially when there are half-priced drinks, as I told you. It's only nine-thirty and we're doing well. What would you like?"

"Just a beer."

"Coming right up."

Chase swung his seat around to watch the people dancing. He noticed Maci's eyes on him. She smiled and then waved. He waved back. Jacob handed him a drink. "That's one gal everyone has tried to connect with, but to no avail."

"She's married."

"No one is sure. There is the possibility she's just watching those kids for him. I dated her for a period of time, and she has to be one of the nicest gals you'll ever run across."

"What happened?"

Jacob rubbed his beard. "I'm not sure, other than one day she said we were done. She never did say what I did wrong, but I was crushed for a bit. Then I met my wife. That took care of that."

Chase took a sip of his beer. "I'm not searching right now for a gal. I have two businesses to operate."

Chapter 19

As he packed his gear for the trip to Whitefish, he wondered why anyone would want the map book.

Chase closed the suitcase. No one could have known about the map in the back cover, so it had to be something inside the book itself. Hopefully, Professor Littrel would have an idea.

He started the thirty-minute drive north to Whitefish. On the way, he thought about what he wanted to achieve out of the weekend. For sure, make a few contacts, as well as finding some books to purchase that the patrons would enjoy, and perhaps help him make a profit.

He had been told that a bookstore was not a profitable venture, so why was he doing this? Simple, to do something his father told him he couldn't do. His father always wanted him to be an attorney but never thought about what Chase wanted in his life. It wasn't being an attorney, since many of the cases he tried involved people who were liars on both sides of the aisle.

Ten minutes later he pulled into the Whitefish

Convention Center parking lot. Entering the book convention, Chase stopped and surveyed all the displays of books that lined a dozen aisles, as well as the several dozen booths set up along the walls.

A soft hand touched his shoulder. Kady peered up at him. "It can be overwhelming for the first time, but this is nothing compared to the big ones. Is there anything specific you're searching for?"

He smiled at Kady. "That's a quandary for me."

She hugged him. "It's good to see you."

"And you too. Let's take a peek up and down the aisles to see what they have, then we can produce a game plan. It'll be a long day." She took his hand.

"What are you doing here?" Chase asked.

"My uncle is hoping to sell a couple of old books, so I decided to join him. Would you like to meet him?"

A man carrying a bag approached them. "That's my uncle right there."

Chase took a deep breath when he saw the man who'd fled from his store. "Another time. Right now, I need to check out the book conference. In addition, I'm scheduled to meet someone."

For the next hour, he browsed the displays and chatted with the sellers, then he found a chair to sit in to write down some thoughts. He didn't know what to think about Kady's uncle. Did she know about him stealing the book? He couldn't imagine she would, but other than the other night, he hadn't talked to her for a couple of years.

The clock read three, so he headed to his meeting with the professor from the University of Montana. He found him in a booth near the back. "Professor Littrel?"

The distinguished man peered up from his reading

with his glasses sitting down his nose. He had dark black hair, parted in the middle, and a beard. The professor seemed younger than Chase had expected. "Yes, I'm Professor Littrel. You must be Chase Connor. Have a seat, and let's take a look at what you have."

Chase pulled the map out of his backpack, handing it to the professor who spread it out on the table. "This is not an old map; it's a recent one. My initial thoughts are this shows the Great Northern Railway route that ran from St. Paul, Minnesota, to Seattle, Washington in the 1800s." He pointed at some dots. "Those are where stopping points were to be, including Kalispell."

He sipped his tea. "However, after studying this map a bit more, I don't believe it involved the railroad company; it involved something else." He placed his finger on different spots that looked like shovels. "If you notice, there are nine of them on the map, many of them in the Smith Lake area." The professor opened up his laptop and started searching. "Here it is. Just as I thought. There was an article in the last month about a missing girl, fifteen, who was last seen in the Smith Lake area with a group of other teenagers." He glanced up at Chase. "Was this map in a book?"

"Yes, it was sewn into the back of an old history book that had maps and historical information about Montana."

"Do you remember how old the book was?"

"It had to be in the late 1800s or early 1900s, but the map seems to be much older."

The professor slapped the table. "You're right, Chase, it does. I'm just speculating here, but what if those shovel signs were actually the spots where bodies are buried?"

Chase's eyes popped up. "Are you saying a killer provided clues to his work? That makes no sense."

"We have to find that book."

Chase sighed. "The book is here. Someone is trying to sell it."

Professor Littrel eyed him. "I don't understand."

"Someone stole it from the bookstore, so he's probably here trying to sell it."

The professor jumped up out of his chair. "Let's find it. This could be a tremendous help."

They ambled around the conference center for the next thirty minutes when Chase stopped in his tracks. "Right there. That's the guy with the book talking to the older man." Chase snapped a photo from his cell phone of the two.

"Good idea," Professor Littrel said. "Let's see what they do."

The two browsed at other kiosks with Chase keeping his eyes on the two men. After a few minutes, after the old man had thumbed through the book, he slammed it down on the table. He said something to the other man that Chase couldn't hear. The old man hurried away from the seller, who took the book, walked over to a booth, and promptly sold the book after a few minutes to the vendor.

"The book's for sale," Chase told Professor Littrel. "Let's grab it before someone else does."

The two made their way over to the book vendor and started browsing through books. Chase found the book he was searching for, purchased it, and then they returned to the professor's table. "Back to the comment about thinking these marks are burial spots, when did it start?"

"I'll have to do some digging—no pun intended—and get back with you on that. Right now, I have to leave, as they want me to give a talk on history books. I'll take a photo of this map, which will give me more time to seek the information I need. Once I do, I'll get back to you."

"Maybe we should just turn it over to the authorities."

The professor stood up. "Let me do some digging first, then I'll take a trip to Mountain Ridge to talk to you about it. Maybe I'll even visit the areas where the graves are located, if that's what they are. Good plan?"

"Good plan."

Chapter 20

At the hotel, after Chase checked in, he grabbed the elevator, pushed the button to the third floor, and found his room. He had a lot of things on his mind, so he decided to soak in the hot tub down by the pool to relax and think.

His eyes opened when he heard the door to the pool open. He glanced at the door seeing Kady and a guy walking in. What were they doing here?

"Do you mind if we join you, Chase?" Kady asked.

Chase scooted up. "Why not?"

The two joined them. "This is my fiancé, Karl Johnson. Karl, this is Chase Connor."

"Ah, the multi-billionaire who decided to hightail it out of California. Nice to meet you."

"Same here."

Kady scooted toward Chase allowing Karl to sit beside her. "Did you find what you were looking for at the book conference?" she asked.

"I did, actually. Tomorrow will be another day, so I hope to find some more."

"What kind of books are you looking for?" Karl

asked.

"Most of the books here are historical, which is a good fit for a portion of my bookstore."

Karl moved to the other side of the hot tub. "Kady told me you were an attorney before you came here. Why a bookstore?"

Chase pulled some suds toward him. "I get that a lot, and what I've told everyone is I want to do something of my own. Many tell me I'm nuts for purchasing a bookstore, but I've found it therapeutic, which I need after a year of enduring the rat race of my father's law firm."

Kady eyed him. "How is it going? Are you profitable?"

"At this point it's been going well, but it's early, plus I'm new. Tell me, when are you two getting married?"

Karl turned to Kady. "You'll have to ask her. She can't make up her mind."

She gave her fiancé a glare. "I'm not sure. We had been shooting for June, but Karl's right, I keep dragging my feet."

"Why?" Chase asked.

Kady took a deep breath. "Something has come up that I need to deal with."

Karl smirked at her. "She just won't tell me what's going on in her mind."

Kady stood up. "I'm going back to the room. Chase, it was good to see you again." She grabbed a towel, dried herself off, then hurried out of the pool without a word to Karl.

He turned to Chase. "I have no idea what's gotten into her these last few weeks. She's just not herself."

"How long have you known Kady?"

Karl thought about it. "A year. It was right after she broke up with a guy she'd been dating for more than a year—a guy she wouldn't say anything to me about. She keeps saying that's her past, and she wants to move forward, but for some reason she still has feelings for the guy."

"Or maybe she's just telling you the truth and wants to move forward."

"You could be right. I should have a conversation with her."

While back in his room, Chase studied the map and then the book. What did they have to do with each other?

He spent the next day buying books, talking to booksellers, and listening to speakers. It was around four when an announcement was made that a major blizzard was about to hit the area in the next fifteen minutes. The roads would be closing.

Many of the people attending the book conference had already driven home before the storm hit. The organizers allowed those stuck in Whitefish to leave their books and other things in the community center until the storm cleared and travel was available.

It was close to five when Chase made the trek back to the hotel. The wind was strong and the snow was coming down hard. He walked through the double doors of the hotel and rubbed his hands, peering at the manager. "There's a lot of snow and wind out there," Chase said.

"I heard that," the manager said. "No driving tonight. I'll be stuck here in the office, but at least there's a comfortable bed."

He headed into his hotel room. It was surprising he didn't see Kady at the book conference, but then maybe she had heard about the blizzard coming in and returned home before it hit. He remembered her when she was twelve, and now at twenty-two, she had grown into a beautiful woman. Karl was a lucky man if he could figure out how to understand her.

Chase snapped his fingers. He grabbed the book, then flipped it to the map in the middle. He viewed the spots and remembered reading that no gold was found at those spots. Next, he placed the map on the bed, looking at the shovels on the map. It sure looked like those spots matched those in the books. He thought for a moment. Could the shovels be where the bodies of those who had been missing were buried? Did someone put together this map to help the authorities find the bodies, if there were any?

The next morning, Chase headed to the front desk where the manager was standing. "Excuse me. Where would you suggest breakfast?"

"There's a cafe down the street that sells buffalo pies. You should try it."

Chase donned his coat and headed down the street toward the cafe the manager had mentioned, then entered the crowded cafe. Chase checked his phone for the time. Ten-thirty. He had been that tired.

A host approached him. "One? Follow me."

He followed the man to a corner seat, then he placed a menu in front of Chase to look over. "I'll be right back."

He studied the menu and chose Ketchum green chilies, sour cream, bacon, cheese, and over easy eggs. Of course, he'd never tried any of them. He closed his menu, surveying the restaurant. Anyone who was there would know the name of the cafe with all those buffalo photos everywhere. He really liked the big painting of the buffalo placed on the layers of bricks.

For some reason the buffalo's staid expression made him think of his own life. What did he want to do with it? For sure, he wanted to get acquainted with the United States, play at a putt-putt course in each state, and camp and hike in a national park in every state. There'd be no children or wife in his future. Being a Connor had knocked that out of him.

His eyes widened as the host brought his meal. "This is going to be a lot of food."

She smiled. "That might be a good thing. With this weather, who knows how long we'll be open."

"Good point."

After breakfast, Chase strolled around Main Street viewing all the Christmas lights as the snow fell and the wind continued blowing. He headed toward the only tourist sight open, Going to the Sun Gallery.

Chase stopped in front of the shop and looked at the sign above the store with a sun in the middle of the four words and a red stripe around the sign. Chase snapped a photo from his cell phone.

When Chase opened the door, a short, stocky lady with gray hair hurried over to them. "Welcome. Thank you for venturing out on such a blizzardy day."

Chase smiled. "I'm surprised you're even open today."

"We had thought about keeping it closed, but we are Montanans, and there are always foolhardy people who like to venture out and can't stay in their homes for one minute."

Chase laughed. "There is that. I was at the book conference yesterday and wound up in the hotel for the evening."

"I've heard that happened to several people, and it's a good thing because the roads are treacherous. My good friend works for the highway patrol, and he said there were at least half a dozen accidents between five and six. He said the roads won't be cleared before tomorrow at the earliest." The lady waved a dismissive hand. "Enough about the weather. How about I give you a tour?"

"That would be wonderful," Chase said. He followed the lady through the gallery.

"As you can see, we have a nice assortment of bead and topaz jewelry, sculptures, and paintings. We are also feature displays of local art and unique pieces, and all of our art captures the Native American culture. An extensive selection of the jewelry is made onsite by the owner."

"This is amazing. I've never seen anything like this. You have a wonderful store," Chase said.

The lady turned toward the door when another couple walked in. "Excuse me. If you have any questions, please feel free to let me know. Enjoy."

Chase ambled through the gallery. He counted at least forty artists represented. Not only were they local and regional, but some were even international. He wandered around for another hour or so before he came to a specific piece of jewelry that caught his eye. A Montana sapphire. He had heard about the gem, revered for its beauty, rarity and full rainbow spectrum of color. Chase turned to the owner. "I'd like to purchase the Montana sapphire."

"Perfect choice for someone who's in love."

He shook his head. "There's no one at this time."

She smiled, carefully placed the ring in a container, and handed it to Chase. "It'll be eleven hundred dollars with tax."

Chase paid with a credit card, then stuffed it in his pocket.

"Here's the receipt," the lady said.

"Thanks, ma'am. You do have a wonderful gallery. Everything is beautiful. Wait, I see something else." He purchased a painting of the view of Glacier National Park. "I've always heard how beautiful this place is."

"Maybe you'll get to see it someday."

Chapter 21

Chase arrived back at Mountain Ridge on Monday morning. He opened the store and was doing some book cataloging when a group of adults walked in. "Can I help you?"

"Yes, we have some books we'd like to sell to you, if you would accept them."

"Let me take a look." He studied the books. "Some interesting titles here, especially the young adult books."

"That's good to know," one of the ladies said. "My daughters have many of these books, so I'll talk to them and find out what are the bestsellers for YA."

"Always interested in new genres, so yes, please let me know."

Ten minutes after they left, Professor Littrel called. "Chase Connor, did you get your fill of books at the conference?"

"It turned out to be a wonderful event, which I learned a lot from, and we figured out some things about the book."

"I did some research, and I have an idea what may

be happening. I'll drive down to Mountain Ridge on Wednesday, if that works for you. If you're up for it, we can do some exploring in a couple of those areas."

Chase sighed. "We received a lot of snow here, so will it still be feasible?"

"It should be because we'll be using GPS coordinates that will give us the exact area, then we can do some shoveling. If you enjoy strenuous work."

Chase laughed. "It'll be something new for me."

Professor Littrel laughed also. "You're becoming a true Montanan."

Once Chase got off the phone, he went back to work cataloging and placing the new books on shelves.

It was close to noon when the door opened. Meredith walked in with two sandwiches and two drinks. "I hope you're hungry," she said, setting the food and drinks on the table.

Chase finished placing a book on an upper shelf, climbed down off the ladder, and grinned at Meredith. "I'm starved."

She sat next to him at a table and surveyed the bookstore. "Sophia is right, you have done a wonderful job." She turned back to Chase. "Sophia told me to stop by to tell you she made it to Boston. She also mentioned bringing you some food because you seem to forget when to stop to eat."

Chase laughed. "Wow, she's figured me out in such a brief time. Is this a day off at the hospital?"

She nodded. "I work the weekend shift, so I usually get a couple of days off during the week. But I have next weekend off since Sophia left, and she passed along her tickets for the yurt outing, meaning you're stuck with me for the weekend."

"I could give you my ticket so you could take Nick with you."

She shook her head. "He's not into those sorts of events."

"How many have you been to?"

"Half a dozen, making me an expert. I'll make sure nothing happens to you."

"I feel better already."

She laughed. "Do you need help this afternoon?"

He shrugged "If it wouldn't be a problem."

"Nope, just tell me what you need from me. I do know a bit about books."

Chase laughed. "Mr. Boer must have told you how I got this business."

"What do you mean?"

He sighed. "He asked me why I wanted to take over his business, and I told him I like to read books."

"And that's why he sold you the business?" Meredith's eyes widened.

Chase took a deep breath. "To be truthful, I believe he would have sold it to the first person who wanted it."

They both turned when the door opened. "Go ahead and get that. I'll start putting books away on the shelves," Meredith said.

Chase smirked. She touched his arm. "I'll figure it out."

"Can I help you?" Chase said to the tall, Native American gal with long black hair and charcoal eyes.

"Are you Chase Connor?"

"I am. And you are?"

"Willa Green. My sister, Tanya Green, is one of the girls who was kidnapped, and I'm hoping you can help me."

"Why me? Have you talked to the sheriff's department?"

She nodded. "They can't help me, but I believe you can."

"If they can't, I don't know what I can do."

She pulled out some pieces of paper. "I've done some research and found that she was last seen above Smith Lake near this area." She pointed to a sketched photo of the lake and some trails.

"Where did you get this?"

"I found it in my sister's room when I was looking through it the other day. Don't know how the officers missed it."

"Excuse me for a moment." Chase disappeared upstairs, grabbed the map, and hustled back downstairs. "Let's take a look at this map and see how this drawing fits with it."

He turned when Meredith joined them. "Willa, how have you been?"

"Meredith, you work here?"

"No, I'm just helping Chase for the afternoon. What brings you here?"

Willa sighed. "I'm hoping Mr. Connor can help me find my sister."

Meredith's eyes lit up. "I'll help any way I can."

They pored over the map and found the place that seemed to tie into the sketch that Willa had. "I think we've found the area where this sketch took place, right here above Smith Lake. There's a shovel, meaning that's where Tanya was taken."

Willa started crying. "So that means she's dead?"

Meredith wrapped her arms around her. "We don't know that. Don't give up hope."

"It gives us a place to start." Chase glanced over at the clock. "It's almost four, so I'm going to close the bookstore. We'll see if we can find this spot."

"I'll help," Meredith said.

"Let's go," Chase said.

They climbed into the Jeep Cherokee and drove toward Smith Lake. Meredith was reading the map. "I think this is the spot, Chase."

He pulled off the road. They stared up at a mountain. "That's a steep climb," Willa said. "What would my sister be doing up there?"

Chase crawled out of the car. "Let's see what we can find out."

They searched around for a trail.

"Over here," Meredith said. The other two joined her. "It's a way up."

Chase led the way, followed by Willa, with Meredith bringing up the rear. They traveled for about fifteen minutes before Chase stopped. He reached into his backpack, pulling out a canteen. "Here, stay hydrated."

Willa took the first gulp, then passed it on to Meredith. Willa eyed Chase. "Why do you carry a backpack?"

Chase sighed. "I'm a California boy, so I'm still trying to get used to the cold. In the backpack I keep clothes to keep me warm if I'm ever stuck, like on a mountaintop."

"Good luck," Willa said. "It's always cold here."

They continued the climb, then an hour later they reached the high point they were looking for. "Let's take a look around here to see what we can find," Chase suggested.

They continued searching the area for the next hour then took a break on a rock.

"Nothing at all," Meredith said. "It's frustrating."

Chase continued scanning the area. "We may not be at the right spot, but this is it for today since it's getting dark. Professor Littrel is joining me from the University of Montana on Wednesday. We can start here."

It was close to eight when they arrived back down the mountain. "Anyone hungry?" Chase asked.

"Yeah, what are you thinking?" Meredith asked.

"The Mountain Ridge Bar & Grill."

They arrived there around eight-thirty. "I'll be right in," Willa said. "I badly need a smoke."

Meredith and Chase walked in and found a place to sit.

"It's always busy in this place," Meredith said.

"I've been here a couple of times, and you're right about it being busy. They have decent food."

Willa joined them, sliding in next to Chase. "I'm sorry, I just needed a cigarette to calm my nerves. I keep wanting to quit, but it hasn't happened yet."

The server showed up. "The special tonight is spaghetti and meatballs, or would you prefer the menu?"

"I'll have the special," Chase said. They all agreed to the same meal.

Meredith surveyed the room. "Isn't that Dr. Boyd and his family?"

Chase turned to where she pointed. "It sure is. I don't know if I've ever seen the family together for a meal outside of the house."

Willa jumped in. "The guy Kady is with—I've

seen before, but I can't place him."

Chase sipped on his water. "That's her fiancé. I guess they're going to be married in June."

Meredith sighed. "Nick wants us to be married in June as well."

"What's wrong with that?" Willa asked.

"I'm not sure if I'm ready to marry him, or any guy for that matter."

Willa grinned. "Now's your chance to talk to him about it."

"What do you mean—" She turned to the voice, belonging to her fiancé.

"Meredith, I thought I'd find you here tonight, or at least I was hoping to. Mr. Connor, it's good to see you once more. And who do we have with you?"

Willa grabbed Chase's hand. "I'm Willa Green, and Chase and I have been dating for a month or so, haven't we, honey?"

Chase was dumbfounded. Willa squeezed his hand. He turned to Meredith's beau. "It doesn't really matter because it seems like just yesterday we got together. Why don't you join us?"

Meredith scooted out. "I need to talk to my fiancé."

Once they left, Chase turned to Willa. "What was that all about?"

She grinned. "I wanted to make sure her fiancé didn't think you two were together."

"We're not together."

She smirked. "My dear Chase, Meredith likes you."

"And you know that, how?"

"Let's just say a woman knows these things."

Chapter 22

On Wednesday, when Professor Littrel arrived at the bookstore around ten-thirty, Chase was waiting on a customer. "I'll be with you in a moment, Professor Littrel," he said.

"No hurry, I'll just browse around the books."

Fifteen minutes later, Chase approached the professor, who was leafing through a book on Napoleon. "Are you ready, Professor Littrel?"

"I am. Are you just going to close the store?"

"Nope, Willa Green should be here any moment to manage it while we're traveling through the mountains."

They both turned as the door opened and Willa hurried in. "I'm sorry, Chase. I had to help my mother with something."

"No problem," Chase said, grabbing the map.

Willa touched Chase's hand. "Be careful."

Chase said, "I will."

~

Willa stood at the door watching as the two climbed into Chase's Jeep, driving off toward the north.

She also noticed a car that pulled out a moment after them. Noting the license number, she hurried over to write it down. Once the car disappeared, she picked up her cell phone to call the sheriff's office.

The sheriff picked up after a few moments. "Sheriff Portal, this is Willa Green."

"Ms. Green, what can I do for you?"

"I'm calling to let you know that a suspicious vehicle is tailing my boyfriend. The vehicle's been there for a couple of days with the guy watching the bookstore."

"Did you get the license number?"

"I did." She read the number off to him.

"We'll look into it."

~

When Chase and Professor Littrel reached Smith Lake, Chase pulled the Jeep Cherokee into a parking spot off the road. "We have to do some hiking now."

The two put on winter coats, grabbed some gear, and started a walk up the path. Chase spoke, "Someone told me there is a cabin up over the other side of the mountain, but I don't see anything right now."

"I don't see a cabin either."

They continued to the top of the mountain, then both stopped when they saw a rundown cabin hiding in a group of trees. Chase started down the path with Professor Littrel following. They stopped and Chase surveyed the area. Nothing there they could see. They walked closer to the cabin when a huge dog jumped out at them.

"What was that?" Professor Littrel asked.

A deep voice came from the nearby thatch of trees. "My German shepherd, Dunk, who doesn't allow strangers in the area. He can't reach you, so he didn't eat you. What are you doing on my property?"

Chase and Professor Littrel turned to view a monster of a man with a long beard and long hair. "You have got to be six-ten easy," Chase said.

"Six-eleven, to be exact. I played basketball at the University of Montana many years ago. Now I live alone in my cabin with my dog."

Professor Littrel patted his glove. "Silas Portal, this is where you disappeared to?"

The big man stared at the professor. "My favorite college professor, Professor Littrel. What are you doing on a mountaintop in the snow?"

"We're searching for a spot that we believe houses a young girl who was kidnapped several weeks ago."

Silas shook his head. "No one crosses over that mountain pass after dark. It's a good thing you're here during the day."

"You know about the kidnapped girl?" Chase asked.

"Are you a cop?"

"No sir, I own the bookstore and antique store in town."

The man looked him over. "Old man Harper is in a wheelchair. You're not in a wheelchair, but then you could have been healed, but then again you're a lot younger than he is."

Chase rubbed his hands. "We could sure do with a cup of coffee?"

The big man eyed him. "Why didn't you say so?" He turned toward the cabin.

Chase glanced at the professor. "Is it safe?"

He grinned. "He's just a big teddy bear."

Chase rolled his eyes as the two followed him into the cabin. Inside, their mouths hung open as they surveyed the trophy mounts lining the walls.

"Close the door," Silas said. "It does get cold here."

Chase reached back, closing the door. "I see you like to hunt."

"No, they were here when I showed up, so I just kept them there. I couldn't harm an animal. They're precious."

The professor noticed the magazines scattered around the cabin. "You also like to read? Chase and I are avid readers."

The behemoth turned to Chase as he finished making the coffee. "That could be why you have a bookstore."

Chase grinned. "I believe the coffee is ready."

The big man put up his hand. "You're my guest. Just have a seat, and I'll take care of it." He brought each of them a cup of coffee, then got one for himself. "I don't have cream or sugar, but I do have vodka." He poured a bit into his coffee. "It makes the coffee taste much better. Would you like some?"

"No thank you," Chase said.

The professor grinned. "I believe I'll have a touch of vodka."

Silas grinned. "Now we're talking, Professor."

"I know the professor, but you, young man, I have no clue who you are."

"Chase Connor."

He eyed Chase. "Why would a multibillionaire's son become a bookstore owner? What did you do to tick your daddy off?"

Chase laughed. "Everyone tells me I'm just plain stupid."

He laughed along. "I would agree with them. Now why are you really up in my neighborhood?"

Professor Littrel put his mug down. "The truth is we're investigating a mystery of lost children in the county. We thought you may know something about what's happening and be able to help us. We realize you have nothing to do with it, but we hope you can help us."

Silas frowned. "You're the first ones who have ever asked me about it. The police officers around here are afraid of their own shadow. They know I'm up here but they haven't set foot on this ground." He sipped his coffee. "There are parties in certain areas along the mountaintop. One is about five hundred yards to the north in a group of rocks that cover the area, so no one can see them. It's been a hot spot for many years. I can't tell you if anyone has been kidnapped because I wouldn't know. You might start there."

Chase took a deep breath. "Why would you tell us that?"

He grinned. "Dunk didn't attack either one of you, so that says you're good people. Anything else?"

"Nope."

"Then I would suggest you take care of your business, then skedaddle down the mountain, but be careful since there are mountain lions and other wild animals roaming at night."

Chase and the professor trudged through the snow toward the area Portal had suggested. "That guy is one big dude," Chase said.

Professor Littrel nodded. "He was a man in the

middle during his basketball career with the Grizzlies. They had some good seasons. An NBA team drafted him, but it didn't pan out, so he moved to the mountains. No one has seen or heard from him for at least twenty years."

Minutes later they arrived at the spot on the map. Chase surveyed the spot. "There's a lot of snow here. Where do we start?"

The professor reached into his bag, pulling out a kit. "This is a miniature GR-100 long-range gold detector. While it's mostly used for detecting minerals, I've found it useful for other things. I've never tried it in the snow, so this will be a test."

Within five minutes the professor was ready to go to work. He searched along an area of rocks for the first five minutes, finding nothing. Then he continued on to other areas for another thirty minutes then stopped. "Nothing." He brushed snow off a rock and sat down. "Chase, pull out the map."

Chase did as asked, and the two studied the coordinates.

"It has to be right around here. We're close," the professor said.

"Let me try it for a bit, Professor." Chase stepped into a clump of rocks, then ran the instrument along them. It started beeping between a group of rocks. The professor jumped up, joining Chase. Chase set the detector down and started digging in the area with his hands. Ten minutes later he reached the ground.

The professor pulled a brush out of his bag and cleaned off the area.

They both saw it at once.

"It's some sort of ring," Chase said, picking it up

and handing it to Professor Littrel, who carefully examined it.

"It's a gold ring." He handed it to Chase who stared intently at it. "Are these initials? It looks like T.G."

Both said her name at the same time. "Tanya Green."

"Could it be?" Chase said.

"It has to be," the professor said. "This is the exact spot of the coordinates. We should call the sheriff's office to let them know. This is a crime scene now."

Chase made the call to the sheriff. Within thirty minutes the sheriff and a crime investigation team arrived. "How did you find this?" Sheriff Portal asked the two.

"It was really the help of your brother," the professor said.

The sheriff's eyes widened. "Silas lives in this area?"

Professor Littrel nodded. "In a cabin back over the mountain a bit."

"I'll be darned. The family wondered where he disappeared to, and he's been right here in our own backyard. Go figure."

They turned to a voice. "Sheriff, we found something else in the digging."

"What is it?"

"A purse or handbag," the deputy said, handing it to Sheriff Portal. He opened the handbag searching through it, then pulled out makeup, a faded identification card, and several other things. "Darn it, I can't make out the name or photo since it's so faded. We'll have to get it back to the lab to see what they can figure out."

It was another hour before the crime investigation team joined the sheriff. "There are no bones in there. The bag and ring are the only items we've found. We'll take them all back to the lab to analyze them."

"Thanks," the sheriff said. Just as the member of the crime investigation team turned away, Chase did a double take on something he saw near the rocks.

"What is it, Chase?" the professor asked.

Chase pointed to an area. "I thought I saw something glittering over there by those rocks."

"Let's check it out," the sheriff said.

They hurried to the area of the rocks where Chase had seen something. They peered around in the snow for a bit. "Nothing?" the sheriff said.

Chase sighed. "There's something here." He continued digging then came across something solid.

"Back off, Chase. Let me take over, since it could be evidence."

Chase stepped back while the sheriff examined the area. "It looks like a container," the sheriff said. He finally was able to pry it up. "It's a box." He opened it to the groans of those who stood around watching.

"Photos. I don't understand," the professor said.

Chase looked closer. "Are they photos of the gals who have been kidnapped?"

The sheriff sorted through them. "You're right. Each photo is of a young gal. This makes no sense. Why nine photos?"

"Oh, no." Chase took a deep breath. "How many girls have been kidnapped in the last year?"

The sheriff pondered the question. "I do believe there are nine girls missing."

Chase pulled out his cell phone and took a picture of the photos and everything else they had found. "Maybe Willa would know something."

Chapter 23

Chase and Professor Littrel arrived back at the bookstore at seven. They followed the aroma of food. "I wonder what's going on," Chase said.

"Chase, dinner is almost ready."

They both peered up at Willa's voice coming from upstairs. The professor tapped Chase on the shoulder. "There's your answer. The young lady cooked us a warm meal."

The two climbed the stairs to the apartment. Willa scurried around the kitchen finishing dinner. She peered at the two. "Grab some seats."

They did as she asked.

She carried in a pot and placed it on the small table. "Beef stew and biscuits with a salad."

"This is a perfect meal for two frozen hikers," the professor said.

"Thank you," Willa said.

The professor turned to Chase after they'd filled their plates. "You really believe that someone is still out there targeting young gals?"

Chase finished swallowing a bite of salad. "It just seems strange that a box full of nine photos would be in that location." He turned and filled Willa in on what they'd found. "What do you think?"

Willa sighed. "It does seem weird that someone would leave a box with nine photos in it, but it may mean the person is leaving clues."

"But why would the person bury photos in a box away from where we found the other items?" Chase asked.

Each of the three stared at each other without an answer. Willa broke the silence. "Why was Tanya's ring there? The ring and the pocketbook belonged to her. Does that mean she's dead? What if she's alive? What if she chose to leave in order to start a new life?"

The professor's mouth dropped. "You're suggesting they ran away to find a better life?"

Chase's eyes lit up. "What are you thinking?"

She took a deep breath. "I'm not going to rule out prostitution or sex trafficking but remember that statistics show that three out of four Native Americans experience violence in their lifetime, but then the same study states that they're ten times more likely to be murdered than any other group."

Chase blew out a breath. "The police will have to take that into consideration."

It was close to nine when the professor said he needed to get back to the hotel to call his wife. "I can drop you off, professor," Chase said.

Chase brought the dishes out to the kitchen to Willa who was sticking them into the dishwasher. "Thank you for all of this. You didn't have to do any of it."

"I wanted to because of what you're doing to help me find my sister." She stopped and peered into his face. "If you want, I could show my gratitude in other ways."

Chase took a deep breath. "I don't know you that well yet."

Throughout the week the bookstore stayed busy with people looking for books and others bringing in books for trade or sale. It was close to five on Friday when Chase finished placing new arrivals on one of the shelves, then turned to survey the interior noticing that every shelf was full.

The door opened. "Mr. Shepherd, can I help you?"

"I thought I'd stop by to see how the town's bookstore is doing."

"We're doing well," Chase said. "Most of the shelves are now packed with books, and the upstairs is completely renovated, but then that isn't why you're really here, is it?"

Nathan's eyebrows furrowed. "Yeah, that's not the reason. I understand you found something up in the mountains the other day."

Chase nodded. "A ring and a pocketbook of sorts, but then you would have known that talking to the sheriff. What are you asking me?"

His chin lifted. "You're new to the area. I'm suggesting you let law enforcement handle what's happening around here."

Chase lifted his chin. "You know what's happening, and you're not doing anything about it."

He glared at Chase. "Just heed my words, and stay out of it. I won't be able to control what will happen to you if you proceed."

Chase took a step closer. "What do you believe would happen to me?"

Nathan shrugged. "It could be anything. My daughter's taken an interest in you, so I told her I'd watch out for you."

"Mr. Shepherd, Sophia is in Boston with Kirby, so she won't have to worry."

"I'm talking about Meredith." He pivoted to walk out of the bookstore but stopped to view the inside. "You've done a wonderful job. Hopefully it'll continue."

It was around six when Chase closed up the bookstore. He headed down to the bar and grill for dinner. While he enjoyed the food, he needed to buy some groceries for the apartment he had moved into a week or so earlier. The bar and grill was full when he strolled in. After dinner, he walked down along the Flathead River. He stopped and noticed a group of people clustered around a lit-up area. Chase ambled over there, stood along the fence, and watched people of all ages ice skating. He watched them for a few moments and had to chuckle when ice skaters fell.

"You think you could do better?"

Chase turned to Meredith's voice. She stood there with Nick. "I'm chuckling because that would be me on the ice."

Nick grinned. "You should try it. We're going skating. You can join us."

Chase shook his head. "I don't think so."

Meredith smiled. "It's actually fun. I skated a lot growing up but not for a few years. C'mon."

They walked to the parking lot, Chase paid for the skates and entrance fee, and they sat down to put on skates.

When Chase had a challenging time tightening his

laces, Meredith tightened them for him. She peered up at him. "Does that feel better?"

"It does. Thanks."

Meredith peered at Nick who was waiting for them. "Go ahead, I'll help Chase."

Chase stepped up and tried to walk on them. "Wow, this is going to be harder than I thought."

"Relax, I'll be right here with you."

She had him put his arm around her shoulder, and the two wobbled out onto the ice rink. "Okay, we'll get out of everyone's way, so you have more room to practice. Grab the wall and edge along the ice rink." Chase did that.

"Watch what I do."

He watched as she glided out onto the ice rink, stopped with her toes, and came back to him. "That looks hard."

"You can do it. Push off the wall and glide forward, but not too far."

Chase tried it and fell flat on his behind. "Ouch, you never said an ice rink was that hard."

Meredith couldn't keep from laughing. "I'm sorry. Here, let me help you up." She bent down and with his help, the two stood up and made it back to the wall. "Okay, try it one more time."

He took a deep breath, pushed off the wall, and glided. He went a little further, then slipped, and fell right back down on his fanny. This time she didn't laugh. She bent down to help him up. "You went farther this time. Excellent job. Let's get you back to the wall."

Once they were back at the wall, he looked at her. "How about I stand here and watch you skate?"

"I'll help you this time. Put your arm on my

shoulder, and I'll guide you."

The two pushed off, and he did better. "You're doing an excellent job. Just take it slowly."

They were out in the middle of the rink when Chase slipped, slid down, and pulled Meredith down on top of him. The two locked eyes. Chase broke the moment. "At least I took the brunt of the fall."

"That you did. Do you want to try once more?"

"I'm sure you have more important things to do than teach me how to ice skate."

"I don't because this is actually pretty fun."

"It's fun watching me fall on my—"

She giggled. "Not that part, but it's cool being out on ice skates for the first time in a while. Come on, I have faith in you."

Meredith helped him up, and they started skating once more. He finally got the hang of it. Sophia let go of him and stayed beside him as he glided along the ice. "You're doing well. See if you can stop."

Chase tried what she had shown him and fell face forward sliding into the wall. She hurried down beside him. "Are you okay?"

He grinned. "My ice-skating days are complete."

They both laughed. She helped him up, and they gripped the boards until they were out of the ice rink. They sat down on a bench and took their skates off.

Chase quipped, "That was actually kind of fun."

"I'm glad you liked it."

"I sucked, but it was worth it."

Meredith touched his hand. "You did surprisingly good for your first time. A couple more lessons and you'll be fine."

Chase rubbed his behind. "Tell my back end that."

Chapter 24

On Saturday morning those who were going to a yurt near Big Fork met at a bus station in Kalispell. Chase boarded the bus and noticed Kady sitting in one of the middle seats. He headed toward her. "You decided to come?"

She nodded. "Meredith gave me her ticket. Join me and I'll explain what's happening." Chase sat down next to her. "Meredith and Nick are on their way to Salt Lake City. She found out earlier this week that she was accepted for a doctoral program at one of the hospitals in Salt Lake City, and Nick's father had wanted him to take over the business. She gave me the ticket, but she didn't say anything about you being on the yurt. I hope this doesn't cause any problems between the two of us."

"What about your fiancé?"

Kady's face scrunched up. "He'll be fine. I plan to enjoy myself. Please do the same."

Once everyone was aboard, the bus started off.

As they headed toward Big Fork, the driver explained to the dozen people in the vehicle what the yurt would consist of. "It's pretty popular in Montana.

The place we're staying at will accommodate eight people with three bunk beds and two trundle beds. Several other cots have been set up. A trundle bed is a low, wheeled bed that is stored under a single bed and can be rolled out for use as another bed." He changed lanes. "A wood stove heats the yurt with the firewood located either just outside of the yurt or right inside near the wood stove. There is also a table, chairs, a propane cook stove, and solar lights, among other items. It's a cozy setup, and the views are gorgeous." He continued. "However, there is no running water, and the toilet facilities consist of an outhouse with a pit toilet."

There were several moans.

It was around three when the bus pulled into Big Fork. The bus driver spoke on his loudspeaker. "We'll stop for gas. If you want to grab something for the weekend, this is your last chance."

The passengers stepped out and went into the convenience store. Chase grabbed all the warm items he could find. He also added some ribs to the items in his arms.

Kady grinned. "Are you preparing for something?"

Chase rolled his eyes. "I expect another blizzard, and I'm going to be ready this time."

She couldn't help but laugh. "I'm sorry, it's just that we're in Montana, and it does get cold here."

"I'm still trying to get used to it."

The bus driver drove onto Jewel Basin Road and five minutes later, the bus turned onto National Forest Road 5392, arriving at the Jewel Basin Yurt around five.

The group entered the rounded facility with a deck around it. They all drew a card to see who would cook and do other chores for the evening.

Chase and Kady pulled the low cards and were designated to grill the hamburgers and hot dogs. Chase had started the grill on the deck, and Kady helped him put on the dogs and burgers. "I've never actually grilled before. It's done by one of our servants," Chase said.

Kady giggled. "I'll show you how to grill."

Chase watched as she flipped over the hamburgers. "That's not too difficult," he said. He flipped over the burgers, and she turned the hot dogs. "I know the bus driver told us about a yurt, but really what is this all about?"

Kady took a deep breath. "Part of the experience is the outdoor activities, but there's also the drinking, storytelling, and other things."

He grinned. "Now that we have that cleared up—"

She laughed, grabbed the food, and walked into the yurt. "Let's eat."

The group sat around the inside eating their lunch and afterward signed up for the different activities for Saturday. It included snowmobiling, cross-country skiing, ice fishing, and mountain climbing. Chase and Kady signed up for snowmobiling and cross-country skiing.

One of the ladies peered over the top of a copy of the magazine, *Scope*. "Listen to this," she said. She read an article which talked about Chase Connor and his fiancée, Sophia, marrying the day after Thanksgiving. "How lucky is that gal?" another gal said. "The guy has a multi-billion-dollar trust fund, and she's got it made in the shade."

Her boyfriend looked at her. "Do you believe everything you read in magazines?"

The gal shrugged. "The *Scope* is a reputable magazine and usually has things right, so yeah, I believe it."

One of the girls asked for the magazine. "I want to see how hot the guy is." She looked at the photo of the two. "Wow, he's one hot person. The gal looks like a model. I'd love to have that body."

"She is a model. At least that's what the story says, and she's going to be one rich gal." The woman's boyfriend turned to Chase. "If you had a nice haircut, that guy could be you."

Chase looked at the photo in the magazine. "It could, but then there are theorists who believe we all have a doppelgänger." Chase listened to them talk for a while and then stepped outside. Five minutes later, Kady joined him.

"Look at the gorgeous sky with all the different colors," Kady said. "And the clouds coming over the snowy peaks."

"Does that mean there's going to be a snowstorm?"

Kady sighed. "Probably a big one."

Chase rolled his eyes. "Great."

Kady sighed. "Was there someone after me you were going to marry?"

"Nope. There was a gal once I was in love with, but I screwed it up."

"Sophia did love you, Chase, but it was better for her to move forward with Kirby."

Chase stared out at the mountains. "It wasn't Sophia; it was another gal."

"Oh, I'm sorry," she said, gently touching his arm. "I'm here to listen if you want to talk about it."

He turned to her. "Someday. Right now, I'm

crashing since we have to get up early to go cross-country skiing."

Everyone went their separate ways after breakfast the next morning. Kady helped Chase into his skis. Chase looked at her. "If I need help putting on a pair of shoes, what's next?"

"We'll just have to see." She grinned.

Chase took a deep breath, stood up, and pushed off the porch. Kady turned to Chase. "Okay, I'll show you an easy way to cross-country ski, so you don't continuously fall into the snow."

"That would be nice."

He watched as Kady explained her technique. "Each ski is pushed forward from the other ski in a striding and gliding motion, and you alternate foot-to-foot. Like this." She showed Chase how to do it.

"It seems like a normal walking step."

"You can think of it that way," Kady said. "But you have to be a little more balanced. Try it."

Chase did just that and he quickly got the hang of it.

"I think we're ready to go," Kady said.

They took off to the north toward the mountains. They had traveled a couple of hundred yards when Kady asked if he was okay.

"Not too bad," Chase said. "This is actually kind of fun."

"I've always enjoyed it, but I haven't done a lot of it lately because I'm involved in other things. Usually, I try to cross-country ski when we get out here, especially if there is a lot of snow around like there is today."

They continued for another hour before they

reached the base of a mountain. They stopped and looked up toward the top of the mountain. Kady said, "This is called Mount Stimson and is more than ten-thousand feet high. I've never climbed it, but others have told me it's a tough one to climb."

"You mountain climb?" Chase asked.

"I have, but I'm not a religious mountain climber. I take it you've never climbed?"

"Haven't even thought about it," Chase said.

"Are you ready to continue?" Kady asked, adjusting her glasses.

Chase set one of his poles into the snow. "Lead the way."

They continued for another hour around the north side of the mountain when it started to snow. Kady stopped. "We should turn back because it looks like a big storm is blowing through."

Chase pointed to the south where they couldn't see anything. "It's already here. It came in quickly."

"It happens in the Rockies all the time. I should have been better prepared."

Chase touched her arm. "Nothing you could have done about it."

She pulled down her glasses and looked at Chase. "I remember you always being this calm."

"I don't know why, but I am. And we should find a place to sit this one out because we're not going anywhere." He pointed to the blinding snow and heavy winds surrounding them. "I thought I saw a cave of sorts just a bit back from where we came from. We can go there."

"Lead the way," Kady said.

"Good idea."

They started back in the direction they came. It was a struggle for the next thirty minutes because they couldn't see right in front of them. Finally, Chase took a step to the left, felt what he was looking for, and climbed into a little shelter belt.

It wasn't a cave, but it had a windbreak that kept the wind and snow from hitting them directly. He pulled Kady toward him, and they found a place to get out of the blizzard.

Once they were settled, Kady looked up at him. "How did you find an opening in this weather?"

"I'm good at remembering things I see, and this looked like a point on the map."

Kady added. "It's a good talent to have."

Chase started to take off his glasses. "I'm really starting to hate blizzards."

The wind was picking up and the two struggled to stay warm. "I'll be right back." Chase climbed up into the rocks behind him.

"Where are you going?"

"To see if there's a better place for us to take cover."

He was gone twenty minutes and came back in a hurry. "I've found something."

"What is it?" Kady asked, rubbing her arms.

"It's a little opening that has an overhand, and we can figure something out to cover the entrance because it's not that large. It's large enough for the two of us to squeeze in and snuggle until this blows over." Chase led the way up the mountain, and fifteen minutes later they were at the entrance. Kady slipped into the opening, followed by Chase. "This should help," Chase said. "We can take things out of our backpacks to keep as much wind out as we can.”

They stuffed the entrance the best they could. “That should help,” Chase said. “Take off your gloves and stick your hands underneath your shirt or pants to help keep them warm.” Chase pulled off Kady’s boots and started gently massaging her feet. “This should help get some circulation back into your feet and warm them up.”

“Wow, that feels wonderful. Thank you.”

Once he finished with Kady, he started on his own.

“I can do that,” Kady said, sliding over and starting gently rubbing them. “Is that okay?”

He nodded. “You’ve always had such soft hands, and it feels good. Are your hands warmer?”

“They are.”

Chase slid next to Kady and wrapped his left arm around her shoulders. “Hopefully we’ll be able to stay warm.”

Kady added. “I’m just glad we found somewhere to get out of the blizzard.”

“Is it always this cold in Montana?” Chase asked.

“It is, and it will get even colder in January and February.”

Chase laughed. “Look at what I get to look forward to.”

A few minutes later, Kady fell asleep while Chase stayed awake listening to the wind blow. It was going to be a cold night, and he just hoped they would get through it all until either the blizzard stopped or someone found them.

It would be difficult for rescuers to find them because they wouldn’t have a clue where they were, and the weather would be a hindrance. Chase had so many thoughts running through his mind about his life and where it was heading, but then that was the reason he was in Montana. He didn't enjoy the wintry weather in Montana, but he loved the beauty that was everywhere, and he was doing activities he never would have considered in California.

Something caught his eye—a sparkling in the snow. He dug it out. A bracelet. He looked closer at it and found the name, Isabelle. Was that the name of another gal who had been kidnapped? He placed it in his pocket and fell asleep.

Chase's eyes popped open immediately when he heard what sounded like snowmobiles. He quickly removed the entrance covering and made his way down the mountain to where he saw the snowmobiles. Chase jumped up and down to gain their attention. Kady must have heard the snowmobiles as well because she was shouting from behind. "I'm down here. Bring the backpacks."

Five minutes later a snowmobile halted at the bottom of the mountain. They grabbed their stuff and made their way down the mountain where the snowmobile rider waved them over.

Kady grinned. "Are we ever glad to see you!"

That evening Chase was out grilling the ribs that he had purchased for everyone. Kady came out to join him. She stood on the railing and looked out at the mountains. "How are you doing?"

"I'm still kind of shaky after yesterday, but I'll be okay."

She peered his way. "I'll never forget what you did for us during the blizzard." She reached up and kissed him gently on the lips. "Thank you." She helped him load the ribs onto plates. "Right now, everyone is hungry for these ribs, so they had better be good."

After dinner, Chase and Kady sat outside on a bench watching it snow. "It's so beautiful," Chase said. "But the wind can just blow away." They enjoyed the peacefulness of the evening until Chase dug in his pocket. "I found something early this morning at the spot where we were."

Her head popped up. "What is it?"

Chase pulled out the bracelet. "It says Isabelle," Chase read.

Kady's eyes lit up. "Isabelle Jung is another girl who was kidnapped. We must have slept in the area where she was kept. We'll have to tell the sheriff's department."

"I'll do that first thing in the morning. Tonight, I'm going to bundle into my blankets to stay warm."

Chapter 25

One of the deputies joined Sheriff Portal. "How does Chase Connor find these photos and jewelry?"

The sheriff took off his glove and rubbed his face as he scanned the area where Chase and Kady had hidden from the blizzard. "I don't know, but I'm sure I'm going to find out when this is all over. He and I are going to have a conversation."

The deputy sighed. "Do you think he had something to do with the kidnapping of the Native American girls?"

"No way. He's not that type of a guy."

The deputy rolled his eyes. "Why? Because he's rich?"

The sheriff glared at his deputy. "No, because the guy has helped us out a couple of times, and if he was the killer or kidnapper, why would he do something stupid like that?"

"Good point, Sheriff. I'll get back to searching for clues."

"Good idea." The sheriff headed over to an area above the rocks where Chase said he and Kady Boyd had spent the night. As the sheriff was searching around the rocks, he stopped when he found something sticking out of the ground. He reached down and dug around it. Another box. He opened it. Inside was only one photo, a photo of Isabelle Jung. Connor and the professor were right. The killer or kidnapper was still in operation.

He picked up the box, placed it in his jacket, and continued investigating the area. After another half hour, he didn't find anything so he called it quits. One thing bothered him. If the girls were dead, why were there no bones or any indication of that happening? They must still be alive.

After the investigation team wrapped up the area, they headed back to Kalispell with nothing but the necklace and box with the photo. On the drive back, Sheriff Portal contacted Professor Littrel. There was no answer, but he left a message for the professor to call him.

Thirty minutes later as the sheriff pulled into the sheriff's department, the professor called him back.

"Sorry, Sheriff, I was in class. What can I do for you?"

The sheriff turned off his squad car. "Professor, Chase Connor found another item from one of the missing Native American girls. We searched the area and found another box."

"Wow, so there is something to Chase's theory."

"What theory?"

"A theory that the kidnapper is still doing his thing and is playing with law enforcement."

The sheriff growled. "Professor Littrel, would you have time to drive to Kalispell to discuss what you think is happening with us? We've been searching for about a year and found nothing, and now within the last couple of weeks, you and Connor have been able to find several items."

"I'd be glad to, Sheriff, and can be up there tonight after classes. Since tomorrow is Friday, I don't have a class to teach, so I'll have more time to help out. I'd suggest that you get Chase Connor involved. Being a lawyer, he has an analytical mind that will help."

"I plan on it. I'll have a hotel room ready for you when you get here. What time do you think you'll arrive?"

"By dinnertime."

"Why don't you join my family for dinner? We can get started right away then. I'll invite Chase over, along with Kady Boyd. She was there at the most recent site."

"Did you say, Boyd?"

"Yes, I did. Why do you ask?"

The professor paused. "It's just in my research I found the name Boyd several times, but I couldn't find a connection to anything other than they were mentioned in some older books."

"That would make sense since her grandfather and relatives further back had a hand in building the county."

"That would make sense, but I believe there's more to it than that. I'll explain when I get there."

After his conversation with the professor, Sheriff Portal restarted his vehicle, backed it out of his spot, then drove toward the bookstore. He pulled into a parking spot behind the bookstore in Mountain Ridge twenty minutes later. The place was busy so he waited for Chase to finish helping a customer.

Once finished, he walked over to the sheriff.

"Sheriff Portal, are you interested in a book?" he grinned. "We have plenty of them."

The sheriff laughed. "I see that. This place has more books than I've ever seen."

Chase nodded. "We've tried hard to give everyone as much variety as we could. What can I do for you?"

"We found another box in the area where you and Kady were stranded during the blizzard."

"Wow. Is it helping?"

"I hope so. Professor Littrel is driving tonight from Missoula to work with us. We'd like you to help out. Would you join us for dinner tonight at my place?"

"I'll be there."

~*

That night, Chase drove to the sheriff's house. Everything seemed to be coming to a head.

After two knocks, the sheriff answered the door. "Welcome, Chase. Everyone else is here. Please join us."

Chase followed him into the living room where he noticed the professor sitting on the couch chatting with Kady's fiancé, Karl, both with a glass of wine.

"Would you like something to drink?" The sheriff asked.

"A glass of wine would be great."

Chase joined the professor and Karl.

"Good to see you again," the professor said, standing up to greet him.

"You too, professor. How was the drive?"

"A storm is heading our way, so I'll be stuck here for a day or so."

"Dinner should be ready in a few moments." The sheriff sat down on a recliner. "Chase, have a seat." He pointed at another recliner.

Chase sat. "Nice and comfortable. What brings you here, Karl?"

"The sheriff invited Kady tonight after you two found the items during the blizzard. I'd like to thank you for saving her life."

"We saved each other's lives. I really hate blizzards."

The professor nodded. "They can be treacherous. You two were extremely fortunate. Many have died in the mountains during blizzards."

"Dinner's ready." They all turned to Kady's voice.

She was wearing a blue dress with knee-high boots, and her brown hair was tinted with blonde hues.

"You look nice tonight," Chase said.

"Thanks," she blushed.

The men sat down around the table, the ladies joining them after bringing out the meal. Kady helped hand out the salads, then sat down.

As they ate their salads, Sheriff Portal started the conversation. "I'm glad you could join us tonight. Professor, Chase, the information the two of you have provided is opening up this case of the missing girls."

"Thanks," Chase said. "But there are some questions that we haven't been able to answer."

"Such as?" the sheriff asked.

Chase pulled out his cell phone and showed the sheriff a photo that he had taken at the recent book conference. "I know this is Dr. Boyd's brother, but this older man—I have no idea who he is."

The sheriff stared at the photo, then handed it over to Louisa. "Oh my," she said. "That's Nathan Shepherd's father."

"He's been dead for five years," the sheriff said.

"It sure looks like him," Louisa said. "The hair color is different, of course, and it looks like he's had some work done with his cheeks, but we both remember the way his eyes look."

Chase interrupted. "What would he have to do with any of this?"

"That's a good question," the sheriff said. He turned to the professor. "You said something about the Shepherds being prominent in your research."

The professor has just finished chewing a piece of his meatloaf. "I did. Amos Shepherd came up several times in the last five years."

Kady's eyes widened. "Amos is the grandfather's name, but he's dead."

"Are you sure?" Chase asked.

She turned to peer into Chase's eyes. "I was at his funeral just before I went to California with Dad."

"That's true," the sheriff said. "However, if I remember right, it was a closed coffin, so we're not really sure if he was in it or not."

Chase pivoted to the professor. "What was the significance of Meredith's grandfather?"

The professor put down his fork. "Over the years the Shepherd family has had an enormous impact on the railroad and the growth of Mountain Ridge. They own a large tract of land in the Smith Lake area, all where the bodies went missing."

Chase frowned. "Do they own land in the area where we found the latest necklace?"

The professor shook his head. "The land belongs to the Boyds."

The sheriff sighed. "Then there is a good chance

that this is Sophia and Meredith's grandfather, or at least someone who looks like him. I'll have a talk with Nathan about this."

After dinner, while Kady helped Louisa clean up, the men went to the den. The sheriff eyed Chase. "Let's see that map you have."

Chase pulled it out of his backpack and rolled it out. He also pulled out the book, turning to the two pages that correlated with the map. Chase explained what he thought. "Each one of these shovels on the map coincide with the gold marks in the book. No gold was ever found in those areas, but it's no coincidence that they match. I just couldn't figure out how, until the professor did his research."

The professor took over. "Every one of those markers is either owned by the Boyds or the Shepherds. In addition, as Chase said, no minerals were found in those areas, but gold was found in the region in either direction, which is strange in itself."

"Maybe they knew about it and used it for something else?" the sheriff said.

"But what?" the professor asked.

The sheriff studied the map once more and pointed to the two sites where they had found evidence. "If we follow the route of the shovels, the one here up north is the first, and this one is the ninth and last. Everywhere in between is another important clue, which makes me believe that if Chase is correct, another kidnapping will occur somewhere in this area."

Chase looked confused.

"Hold it," the professor said. "The sheriff could be right." He grabbed one of the several books he had brought and flipped to a page that he had marked.

"Right here. About twenty years ago, the Boyds purchased some land right in that area. If you look at the old book that Chase has, it shows one of those gold markers right there," he said, pointing to the spot.

"If that's the case, then that is where the next kidnapping will take place. But are the Native Americans dead or not?"

The three stared at each other, clearly not sure what to think. Chase finally broke the silence. "We have to go with the assumption that they're still alive, only because you haven't found any bones."

"How deep have you dug, sheriff?" the professor asked.

"Maybe five feet."

The professor shook his head. "Then if there aren't any bones, then there probably aren't bodies since killers usually bury bodies shallow. However, it may not be deep enough if they had the time and equipment. Can you get your hands on a rotary cutter or hydraulic ripper to break through the frozen ground?"

"I'm sure we can," the sheriff said.

They turned when the gals came out with iced tea. Kady pulled up a chair next to Karl. Once she was settled, she placed her hand on Karl's leg. "Have you found the girls, Chase?"

Chase shrugged. "We're making headway. Do you know anyone who may have a rotary cutter or hydraulic ripper?"

"Sure. Mr. Leopold, the guy who remodeled your apartment, works with all kinds of equipment. I can call him right now if you wish."

"Thanks," the sheriff said. "Here's the plan, but I'll need your help, Chase, Professor."

They both nodded. "Whatever we can do," the professor said.

The sheriff took a deep breath. "I'm sending a deputy with you two, and I want you to check out each one of those sites to see what you can find. In the meantime, Kady, if you can get Mr. Leopold to the sheriff's office, we'll start digging in that area around Smith Lake to see if we can find any bones."

Chapter 26

The next morning Chase and Professor Littrel set out for the first of seven markers to do some searching while the sheriff drove to talk to Nathan Shepherd. Chase and the professor arrived at the second location which was near the community of Creston, established in 1889, according to the sign.

After viewing the map, they found the spot where the next items should be. They dug for an hour before Chase found something hard. He dug around it and found another box, much like the other two boxes they had found. He pulled it out, opened it up, and there were two photos in it.

"The second site," the professor said.

They continued digging for anything else they could find. The professor found a set of earrings and examined them closely, but there were no initials on them. After another thirty minutes, they called it quits, then drove toward the next site near the town of Somers.

As they pulled into the area, the professor pointed out, "There was a lumber mill here that was used for the

Great Northern Railway. They provided more than six hundred thousand logs per year and had built than 120 homes, meaning Somers was a company town."

They pulled into a driveway near their next site. Chase peered up from the map. "It looks like we have a little walk ahead of us," he said. "Are you ready to do it?" The professor nodded.

After a twenty-minute walk, they arrived at their destination. "The scene seems to be a bit different than the others as there are not as many rocks," Professor Littrel commented. "It's just an open area around here."

Chase stopped and peered at the professor. "Is that of any significance?"

"I'll have to think about it."

An hour had passed, and they still hadn't found anything. Chase dropped down on a rock. "Could we be off a bit here?"

The professor looked at the map and the piece of equipment. "According to everything. we're right where we should be."

Chase sighed, then his eyes landed on something sparkling. "What's that?" He hurried over to where he saw the sparkle, reached down, and dug with his hands. He pulled out a colorful object. "A hair clasp. That's new," he said.

The professor nodded. Chase handed it to him and while the professor studied it, Chase continued looking for other items. "Found the box. It was buried right near the item." Chase dug for another fifteen minutes. "That seems to be it."

After they got into the car, they drove toward Mountain Ridge. Chase dropped a question. "Doesn't it seem strange that the only items we find are boxes and women's items? It seems like they're toying with us."

The professor sipped on his coffee. "It does make you wonder. I'll call the sheriff."

He put the sheriff on the speaker phone after he answered. "Any luck?" the sheriff asked.

The professor explained what they had found. "What about your conversation with Shepherd?"

The sheriff sighed. "Nathan Shepherd explained that he knew about his father being alive but didn't know anything about the missing girls. Nothing is making sense."

"We agree with that," the professor said. "Same two type of items: a box and a hair clasp."

Chase interrupted. "How can you explain a guy faking his death? It only means he has something to hide."

"That's a good thought," the sheriff said.

"Were they able to find any prints or anything on what we've given them?"

"I haven't heard back yet, but hopefully they will find something. One good thing is we haven't found the bodies, so that may mean they're still alive. I'll head out to the dig site while you two continue your site visits."

That afternoon Chase and the professor visited three other sites and found the same items: a box and women's items. "We still have three more sites to visit," Chase said. "We'll have to finish them tomorrow."

"I agree," the professor said. "I'm starving. The sandwich and chips just don't cut it, but it is good for my weight. You wouldn't have to worry about that."

Chase laughed. "Give it time."

As they drove back toward Mountain Ridge. Kady called. "I found out some information today. Can you two stop by my apartment? Have you eaten?"

"No, and the professor is starving."

Kady laughed. "How far out are you?"

"It'll be another half hour."

"I'll have something ready for the two of you."

Once Chase closed his cell phone, he turned to the professor. "Kady has information for us, and she will have dinner ready when we get there."

"Great because I'm starving."

"That makes two of us."

After they arrived, Chase knocked on Kady's apartment door, and she let them in. "I hope you're hungry because I grabbed a bucket full of chicken with potato salad and biscuits."

The professor grinned. "That sounds wonderful."

They sat down at the table and dug into the container of chicken.

"Any luck?" Kady asked.

Chase sighed. "At each site, we found a box and a girl's item but nothing more."

Kady finished eating a piece of chicken. "I have some news. I contacted Mr. Grant from the school district today, and I showed him the book. He told me that a guy named Jeremiah Pfarr owned the book, and one day after Tanya Green was kidnapped, he tried to sell the book to Grant, knowing he was a lover of historical books. He didn't buy it because he had so many of those types of books." Kady took a deep breath. "However, he asked Pfarr where he got the book, and he said it was from an older gentleman who told him it was worth a lot of money. He didn't get the man's name but bought the book for ten dollars."

Chase eyed Kady. "Did he ask the man if it was worth so much, why would he sell it for ten dollars?"

"He needed the money for a pack of cigarettes was all the old man said. The old man was never heard from again."

The professor frowned. "This is getting weirder and weirder."

Kady peered at the two. "The Shepherds want us to join them tonight. They didn't say why, but it sounds like others will be there at seven-thirty. The only time the Shepherds do anything this quickly is when they have something important to tell everyone or show everyone. Something that makes them stick out."

The professor stood up. "I should get back to the hotel, get a shower, and I'll meet you two at the Shepherds."

Chase turned to the professor. "I'll meet you at the car." Once he stepped out, Chase turned to Kady. "Thank you for all of your help and especially the dinner."

She peered into his eyes. "You seem frustrated."

"I'm a bookseller not a detective."

She winked. "You're good at both."

Chapter 27

Chase and the professor stood watching all the people mingling in the Shepherd household. Willis and Allison joined them.

Willis grinned. "I'm sure you're used to these kinds of outings in California."

"Yeah, I've been to a few."

The professor piped up, "Do you have any clue what's happening?"

"Your guess is as good as mine," Willis said, grabbing Allison's hand.

They peered up as Dr. Boyd joined them. "Isn't this exciting?"

"What's exciting?" Chase asked.

Dr. Boyd's eyes went wide. "You really don't have any clue?"

He shook his head.

"You'll find out in a few moments then."

Willis and Allison asked the professor to join them to meet a few people. After they left, Chase took a chance. "Dr. Boyd, do you know anything about those missing girls?" Chase noticed hesitation before Dr.

Boyd spoke.

"I know as much about what is happening as you do, Chase. Why do you ask?"

"I saw your brother give a book to an older man at the book conference. The book that was stolen out of the bookstore."

Boyd frowned. "That doesn't mean he stole it."

Chase sighed. "Come on, Dr. Boyd, the chances are he did or knows who stole it. More importantly, what is his connection to these young girls? You know what's going on."

Dr. Boyd lowered his voice. "Chase, stay away from things you don't know about." He then pasted on a smile. "Let's enjoy what's about to happen."

They headed over to an area with a makeshift podium where the guests were gathering.

Nathan Shepherd walked up to the podium. "Welcome, everyone. Tonight is a wonderful night in Mountain Ridge. Before I provide you the exciting news, I'll introduce a couple of people who have made it possible."

He introduced several county commissioners, a few state senators and representatives, along with several financial wizards. "We all know these people well. Now I'd like to introduce two people who have put the final pieces into this project. Micah Connor and Peter Drake, who work for Connors and Associates in California."

Nathan took a sip of his glass of wine. "The company is providing more than fifty percent of the investment for Mountain Ridge Resorts, which will be located above Smith Lake. It will consist of a two-hundred room resort with many outdoor recreation activities, a hot tub, a ballroom, and much more. All the permits have been completed, and it's a go."

Everyone clapped to hear the news. They all turned to the sheriff and his crew who walked in.

"Sheriff Portal, you're interrupting an important event," Nathan Shepherd said.

"Am I now?" he said. "I've come to arrest you, Nathan Shepherd, for the kidnapping and possible murder of nine Native American girls in the county."

Gasps ensued throughout the room.

"Sheriff, you have no idea what you're doing."

"Don't I? By the way, do you know where your father is? He's also under arrest, as is Dr. Boyd and his brother, along with several others."

Micah interrupted, "Mr. Shepherd, my father would never work with people who are doing illegal things, so we'll be pulling our investment out."

"We have an agreement," Nathan Shepherd said.

"Yes, we've signed the agreement, but if you read the fine print, it states we can pull our money if anyone is involved with any illegal doings, and kidnapping and possible murder are about as illegal as can be."

Everyone watched in horror as they hauled the three out of the house. Ophelia ran after her husband glaring at the sheriff. "You're done in Flathead County."

Micah walked over to Chase who shook his hand. "Thanks, Micah."

"No problem, little brother. You were right all along that the Boyds and Shepherds had something to do with the kidnapping. We have a promising idea where the girls are and hope to get them back within the next couple of days. They're all alive, which is a good thing."

The next day Chase joined the others who gathered around to welcome the Native American girls home. The Boyds had kidnapped them to ship to California to sell to human traffickers who ran brothels and prostitution rings.

Sheriff Portal stood in front of a podium on the steps of the law enforcement center. "We were fortunate they weren't shipped off. There were plans to kidnap another woman on December thirteenth, which is today. The book and map that Chase Connor found helped us solve this case. And we couldn't have done it without the help of University of Montana's Professor Littrel."

The crowd applauded.

"Nathan Shepherd has been released for lack of evidence, but Dr. Boyd and his brother are in custody charged with nine counts of kidnapping and nine counts of human trafficking. If convicted, they will spend a long time in prison. Most importantly all the girls are home with their families."

Chase leaned against a wall watching the girls mingle with their family members.

Willa Green noticed Chase and hurried over to him with a young girl. "This is Tanya, my little sister. Thank you so much for what you've done to help all of us. I don't know if Tanya would have been found in time if you hadn't pushed it."

Tanya peered up at Chase. "Will you join us for a celebration meal this afternoon?"

Chase smiled. "Sure, I will. What time and where?"

Once the two left, Sheriff Portal joined him. "Quite

nice to see all this."

"It is, Sheriff. It took a lot of effort of many people, but it was done. How did Shepherd get out of it? We both know he was part of the operation."

The sheriff sighed. "I have to go by evidence, and there was none to keep him locked up. After everyone testified, he came out in the clear. Who lied and who didn't, I have no idea. But right now, we know that the Boyds are involved. I'm sure more will come out if there's a trial. You're an attorney, so you know how these things can turn out."

"Yeah, I'm going to stick with selling books."

The sheriff laughed. "You do that. Again, thanks for what you've done to help solve this."

"No problem. I'll talk to you later." Chase made it back to the bookstore right after lunch. He opened the door, walked inside, then looked around. It was going better than he had ever expected.

He turned when the bell tinkled over the door. "Can I help you?"

An older lady smiled. "I'm searching for some books." A constant stream of customers kept him busy all afternoon.

It was five when Chase closed the bookstore so he could join the Greens' celebration. He didn't really want to join them, but he told the young girl he would do that. Chase locked the door but turned when three kids went screaming by him.

"I'm so sorry," a woman who trailed them said, "They're in a hurry to see their grandparents."

"Your children?"

"Oh gosh no, my sister's. I'm watching them while she and her husband spend a peaceful night together. I should go before they terrorize the antique store. Nice meeting you."

"You also."

Chase made his way to the Green celebration where there were tons of balloons, cake, drinks, and food.

Tanya ran over to him when she saw him. "I'm glad you could make it, Mr. Connor," she said. "Come and meet my mother." She took his hand and pulled him over toward a group of people that included a lady with long black hair, bent glasses, and a long-sleeved shirt. "Mom, this is Chase Connor. He's the guy Willa and I were telling you about."

"Oh my, Mr. Connor, we're so glad to meet you. You saved my baby. Thank you."

"Ma'am, there was a group of people who helped find the girls."

She puffed on her cigarette. "I understand, but Willa told me it was you who got the ball rolling. Please join us for some cake and beer if you choose. We also have sodas."

"Thank you." He turned and noticed Willa talking to a couple of guys. He went over to the table to grab some cake and a soda then stood to the side eating it.

Willa joined him. "I'm glad you could make it. Mother was worried about you showing up."

"Why would that be?"

"You're a Connor, and not many of the Blackfeet nation have good things to say about the Connors."

"I don't understand."

She sipped on her beer. "They're the ones who wish to build a resort on Blackfeet land, not near Smith Lake. You knew nothing about it?"

"I didn't, but I'm not involved with my folks anymore."

She blew a smoke ring. "I'm sure the bookstore keeps you busy."

"It does. What do you do?"

"I work with the Native American children in the schools on the reservation. I teach them reading, writing, and speech. It's enjoyable working with them."

"That has to be a rewarding job."

She blew out another ring of smoke. "It is. I'm looking for more in my life though. I'm not sure what at this point. I dated a guy for several years, then he just decided he had enough of me. Bam, just like that he was gone. I never knew what happened to him. Guess It was for the best," Willa said, putting her cigarette out on the ground. "It's a filthy habit I have to stop. There's a part of me that figures that's a big reason guys are turned off—because I smoke. Then again, I'm Native American, and that makes it difficult for many guys to deal with."

Chase sipped on his soda. "You're full Blackfeet?"

"No, I'm thirty percent. The other seventy percent is Canadian. My father is from Alberta. I never see him anymore. As you can tell I'm not as dark-skinned as other Blackfeet." She pulled out another cigarette from her back pocket and lit it up. "As you can tell, I do a lot of smoking, probably at least a pack a day. I also have too much to drink, another vice I'm working to control." She tapped the ashes onto the ground. "Why am I telling you any of this? After today I'll never see you again anyway, and that's too bad because you're the first guy I've ever met who I think I could care about."

Chapter 28

Throughout the week, Chase stayed busy at the bookstore. Friday afternoon he dialed Willa's cell phone. She answered on the third ring.

"Chase, I'm working. I'll call you back when I get a break."

"I'm sorry." He hung up the cell phone and went back to work. Around two, a group of older ladies walked in. "Can I help you, ladies?"

The women glanced at each other but said nothing until one of the ladies dressed in green with gray hair spoke, "We wondered if you would be willing to speak at one of our upcoming senior citizen events at the center?"

Chase peered at them. "I'm honored, but I'm not sure why you're asking me to speak at the senior citizen's center, or what topic you would like me to talk about."

The lady took a deep breath. "You're a fascinating individual who helped find those young girls. Our senior citizens' families will also be there, so we try to have a guest speaker from the area to tell them their stories. It works out well."

Chase shrugged. "I'd be glad to. When would you like me there?"

It was three-thirty when Willa called back. "I'm sorry, Chase, I was in the middle of helping with game day."

"I'm sorry to bother you at work. I should have known better."

"It's okay. What is it you want?"

"I know this is short notice, but would you like to join me for dinner tonight at the bar and grill, then go dancing after?"

There was a pause, then, "I'd love to."

"You would?"

"Of course, I would. What time do you want to meet?"

"The bookstore closes at seven, so say seven-thirty."

"I'll be there."

Chase finished the day, locked up the bookstore, then dropped off the money bag in the bank deposit. He had profited close to five hundred dollars for the week, which was one of his best weeks. Chase arrived at the bar and grill a few moments after seven-thirty. He stepped inside and noticed how busy it was. Once he found Willa sitting in a booth, he hurried over to her and slid into the seat across from her. "Sorry, I'm late."

"I just got here myself."

Chase eyed her. "You look gorgeous."

She blushed. "Thanks. This is the first time I've dressed up like this…ever, I believe."

Chase frowned. "Here I'm wearing jeans and a shirt, while you're wearing a skirt and blouse with knee-high boots."

She peered at him. "How do you know I'm wearing knee-high boots?"

"I noticed them when I sat down. Your legs were crossed."

They turned to the server. "The special tonight is cheeseburgers and french fries."

Chase said, "Are you good with that?"

"Sounds wonderful."

"We'll have the special with a couple of beers. If that's okay, Willa."

"I'm good with that."

Once the server left, Willa turned to Chase. "How was your week?"

"Busy. I made a profit of almost five hundred dollars this week, which is the best I've done since I started."

Her eyes lit up. "That's amazing. Are there certain books people are gravitating to?"

Chase sipped on his beer that had just been delivered. "The most popular genres are Young Adult, history, and mystery. There have been a lot of young people coming in to purchase books, which is surprising according to what Mr. Boer said."

Willa set her beer down. "YA books are popular around the country and are just making their way to Montana. You may have a surge on those types of books over the next few weeks."

"Good to know."

Willa peered around the room then back to Chase. "Why did you ask me out tonight?"

"You're a nice-looking gal, Willa, and I wanted to get to know you better. To be truthful, I've had bad luck with gals. Many are interested in me because I have a lot of money, but that isn't what I want. I want them to go out with me because of who I am."

Willa sighed. "I can understand that because many guys want to go out with me because I'm Native American."

"I don't understand what that means."

She surveyed around the room. "Many think all Native American women are easy."

Chase reached over and grabbed Willa's hands. "Sorry you feel that way. I don't feel that way at all. I see you as an intelligent, beautiful gal who has a future ahead of her. You just need to believe in yourself."

They turned as their meal were delivered. Once the server left, Willa turned back to Chase. "Thank you for that. No one has ever told me anything like that before."

After they finished their meals, Chase stood up. "Would you like to dance?"

She blushed. "I may not be very good."

Chase grinned. "Join the crowd." The two spent the next two hours dancing and chatting. It was after ten when they left the dance floor.

"I had a wonderful evening," Willa said. "I hope we can do this again." She wrapped her arms around him and kissed him gently on the lips.

"I have to give a talk at the senior citizen's center on Wednesday night. Would you like to join me?"

"I'd love to. Good night."

Chase took her in his arms kissing her once more. When she responded, he said, "I'm sorry I shouldn't have done that."

She gazed into his eyes. "Why? It's natural for a guy and gal to do such things."

"I know but how about we just find a nice place to sit and talk? Then see where it takes us from there."

"I'm agreeable to that."

The two found a corner seat in the grill to sit. She searched the room. "Since I was fifteen, I've smoked, drank, had sex."

Chase started to say something, but she put her finger to his lips. "Please let me finish. This is the first time I've been able to express my true feelings because I feel comfortable saying anything around you." She took a deep breath. "Now I wonder why I'm here with you when twice before you told me no. I'm talking to you because I care about you, but my feeling is you're here to fill an urge like any other guy I've been with. Then there's Meredith Shepherd who also cares about you. Because of who I am, she'll end up being the one in your life." She started to get up. "I should go."

Chase gently touched her arm. "I never thought like that. I have too many issues in my life that I'm trying to control. It's past one and we should be getting out of here. If you want you can stay at my apartment since I have an extra bed."

"Are you sure?" she asked.

"Positive. Nothing will happen."

The next morning Chase woke up smelling bacon. Willa turned when she heard Chase come into the kitchen. She peered into his eyes. "Breakfast is almost ready."

"It smells good. What is it?"

"It's called a sheepherder's breakfast—bacon, onion, and hashed brown potatoes. I hope you like it. I also hope it's okay that I wore one of your t-shirts."

He turned her around and peered into her eyes.

"You look marvelous in the t-shirt."

She blushed and tapped him gently on the shoulder. "Breakfast is ready."

After they finished breakfast, Chase took care of some things then started to head down to the bookstore. "Take all the time you need."

Fifteen minutes later, Willa came down the stairs in her clothes from the night before. "I should go now," she said. "I have a lot to think about. Don't know where this will go, but I do thank you for allowing me to speak freely, something no one has ever done before."

Chase wrapped his arms around her neck. "I hope we can do more things together. I know you're worried about Meredith, but I don't see any reason you should be, since she left with Nick, and they're on their way to Salt Lake City."

Willa sighed. "I didn't know that. I'll meet you Wednesday at the senior citizen's center."

"No, Willa, I'll pick you up at your house."

Her eyes widened. "No guy has ever picked me up at my house. Are you sure?"

"Positive." He kissed her gently on the lips. "I hope I can talk to you again."

Chapter 29

Saturday evening, Chase strolled toward the bar and grill thinking about what was happening in his life with the businesses, the gals he knew, and other things. He would hope for the best, but he wouldn't be disappointed at the worst.

Once he stepped into the bar and grill, he found it was packed and there was no place to sit. Finally, he noticed a seat at the end of the bar which he quickly grabbed.

"Chase Connor, where have you been?"

"Jake, I've been busy at the bookstore."

He handed Chase a beer. "I hope you feel up to this right now."

"I could taste it all the way over here. Also, could you make me one of those meatball subs you have?"

"Coming right up."

Chase sipped on his beer watching those on the dance floor, as well as all the people mingling at the tables. Jake brought him his sub.

"What's happening with the antique store?"

"It's still being remodeled. Should hopefully be

ready after the first of the year. On another note, is this the busiest this place has ever been?"

"Oh yeah," Jake said. "It gets this way when they know a horrible blizzard is coming, and they're predicting as much as twenty inches of snow with 40 to 50 mile-per-hour winds to go along with it. If you get stranded in this stuff, forget it."

Chase finished his beer. "I should really think about moving back to California."

Jake laughed. "Many people here would miss you."

"Not likely."

After Jake left to serve others, Chase surveyed the room once more. He saw Kady with her fiancé, along with Willis and Allison. They were having fun. Chase was finishing off his sub when the door opened and the chilly air blew in.

Sheriff Portal walked in with a guy who looked like he was frozen to death. Jake hurried over to help him with Chase right behind.

The sheriff blew out a breath. "There is a blizzard out there. You can't see a foot in front of you, and this one ran into a heavy snowdrift. There must be as many as twelve inches out there already and more coming. He claims his girlfriend and baby are still out there, but I couldn't find them and brought him here because it was the safest place."

"We'll help him out," Jake said, turning to one of his hosts. "We need some warm coffee and some blankets to help him warm up."

Kady hurried over. "Sheriff, I can help."

The man was shaking and started talking. "My girlfriend and our baby are still out there," he said. "Please help them?"

Sheriff Portal tried to calm him down. "There's nothing we can do right now. Hopefully, they found somewhere safe to ride out the storm."

The young man glared at him. "You won't help because she's Native American."

"I didn't know she was Native American until you just told me, but it wouldn't matter. What matters is that the blizzard is horrible, and as you could tell, you can't see anything in front of you. We'll do what we can to help you, and when the blizzard lets up, we'll do what we can to find her."

Chase jumped in. "Where did you find them, Sheriff?"

"About a mile outside of town toward the lake."

The young man spoke up. "I told her to wait in the car while I went for help. The car is just below the mountain road heading up to the cabin, and the car is running."

"That's close to a mile away from here." Chase raced over to grab his coat.

"Chase, you can't go out there. You'll freeze to death." Kady touched his arm.

"The woman has a baby and needs help."

"I'm coming with you," the sheriff said, grabbing his coat and hat.

Chase looked at the guy. "Do you have a better description of where the car is?"

The guy explained to him where they were. "You did the right thing keeping them in the car."

Jake hurried over to the two guys. "Here's some hot coffee to help you out and the young girl. Please be careful."

They climbed into the sheriff's vehicle. It was a

struggle to see because of the strong wind and blinding snow. They would stop every few moments to allow Chase to jump out to clean off the side windows and front one.

The sheriff growled at the second stop. "This was really a stupid idea, you realize that, Chase?"

"Tell me about it," Chase said.

It was twenty minutes before they finally arrived at the area where the guy said the gal and the baby were. His ears perked up.

"It sounds like crying—a baby crying," Chase said. He quickly moved toward the direction the crying came from but had a challenging time seeing where he was going. He stopped when he ran into something covered in snow.

"The car," the sheriff said.

They started scooping the snow off the car and found the front door. The sheriff struggled but finally got the car door open. Chase crawled into the car and saw a young woman with her eyes closed and a baby almost blue with cold. The baby was crying, and the girl looked like she was frozen.

Her eyes opened. "Please save my baby?" she whispered.

Chase turned to the sheriff. "They're alive but barely."

The sheriff helped Chase bring the baby out first, then the young girl. They placed them in the cab of the pickup, wrapped the two in a blanket to keep them warm, and drove slowly back to the bar and grill.

Chase turned to the young girl. "Hold your baby tight because we're taking you somewhere warm."

"Is my baby going to die?"

"You're baby's going to be fine, young lady," Chase said.

It was around one when they finally arrived at the bar and grill. Chase carried the young girl and her baby in. The first person he met was Kady who touched his arm. "Are you okay?"

He nodded. "She's going to be fine."

"I'm so glad. We were all worried."

Chase smiled. "Thanks."

"Here, let me take the baby, and you bring the young girl to the back bedroom with her boyfriend. There are a lot of people in there and even more in the community center. You were the last one to get here out of the blizzard, but no one was hurt or anything."

"That's good to hear."

After everyone had settled in, Chase found a wall, sliding down to the floor. Kady stood above him. "Is there anything I can get you?"

"I could really go for something warm to drink," Chase said.

"I'll get us some hot chocolate."

Kady brought the drinks then sat down next to him. "What were you thinking going out in that weather?"

Chase eyed her. "She needed help. It's the least I can do."

She took a deep breath. "That's two blizzards you've saved someone's life: the first mine, now this young girl and her baby. This is not Chase Connor. What is going on with you?"

Chase sighed. "I'm trying to be a better person, Kady. I blew it with you, and I'll never forget it, which means I have to do a better job."

Kady eyed him. "I always kept our relationship

quiet. You still love me?"

Chase avoided her eyes for a moment than returned them to hers. "You're engaged to marry another man."

Chase's eyes popped open when he heard people stirring around in the bar and grill. Jake brought out some coffee to Chase. "The blizzards not quite finished outside, but we do need help inside."

Chase searched the bar and grill. "Where's the sheriff?"

Jake sipped on his coffee. "He's out locating stranded motorists. Chase, there are three families just on the outskirts of Mountain Ridge that he asked if you would check on."

"I can do that."

Kady sat up and stretched her arms. "I'll help you, Chase."

"Whoa," Karl said, jumping off his seat. "You don't need to do that."

Kady eyed Karl. "I can help. I want to help."

"I really don't like this idea."

Kady touched her fiancé's arm. "I'll be fine. Chase will make sure nothing happens to me." She turned to Chase. "I'm ready when you are."

After they donned their warm coats. boots, gloves, and hats, Jake gave Kady a piece of paper. "Here is a list of people we know of who live in the community. The highlighted names are the three we're not sure about, so start with those three."

Kady's eyes peered up at Jake. "These three are all outside of Mountain Ridge. I thought the sheriff's department had rounded everyone up?"

"They couldn't reach these three, so we're not sure what's happened to them."

"Here, this should help you." One of Jake's hosts came out with some hot coffee and a couple of donuts for the two, along with other supplies the two stuck in their backpacks.

"Thanks," Chase said. Once outside, Chase handed Kady the backpacks and cleared off the windows of the Jeep. Kady did what she could also. "I'm amazed with all the snow, you're not buried in."

Chase shook his head. "I've given up figuring out this snow in Montana." The snow was still falling and the wind was blowing. "Wow, does it always get this cold?" Chase asked.

"It can get colder at times. Let's go."

Chase opened the door and helped Kady into the Jeep. Once he got the Jeep started, they slowly drove outside of town. "Do you know where these houses are?" Chase asked.

"I know of two of them," she said. "The third one is a little further out and in a difficult location. The family are perfect Montanans."

"What do you mean?"

"They want their freedom, and they don't want anyone to bother them."

He cut her a quick sideways glance. "Then why are we doing this?"

She shrugged. "Because the sheriff cares about his county and will do what he can to protect the people."

"I figured that out."

They continued along the streets, stopping at several houses to make sure the residents didn't need anything, but everyone was doing well. The wind ceased its furor as they reached the outskirts of town. "Have you talked to your father?"

Kady searched outside the window. "He's having a challenging time dealing with the charges involved with the kidnapping of the Native American girls. He doesn't admit to any of it, but there is a part of me that believes he did it or was involved with his brother. His brother was always a problem for the family." She turned to Chase. "He's asked for you to represent him in court."

Chase took a deep breath. "I can't because he was willingly involved. And if I took the case, it would go against everything I'm trying to do here."

"I told Dad you wouldn't so he's hired your father to get him off."

Chase shook his head. "Your father will be free soon." He switched the subject. "Are you and Karl still tying the knot in June?"

"It seems like it. Are you dating anyone?"

Chase laughed. "I've had bad luck with gals lately. I have a date with Willa Green on Wednesday at a senior citizen's center event, but I have a feeling she won't be there."

Kady pointed out the window. "Here's our first house."

Chase knocked on the door, and a few moments later an older lady answered the door. "Can I help you?"

Kady spoke up. "We were checking to see if you needed anything after the blizzard struck."

"No, we're good, thank you. It's nice of you two to check on us, but we're always prepared for a Montana blizzard."

"Aren't we all?" Kady said. "We'll leave you alone."

They drove up the road to the next house with the same result. The family was doing okay and the kids were outside building a snowman in the snow. The kids stopped what they were doing and talked to Chase and Kady before their parents came out and joined them. They chatted, then the duo were on their way to the final house.

"This house is spooky to me." The old house had broken windows in many places, a door that was barely hanging on its hinges, and cobwebs in different areas of the house.

"What do you mean?" Chase asked.

"I don't know, it's just that everyone has heard about weird happenings out here. One time people thought they saw ghosts, another time someone heard moaning in the night, and then there was the mysterious disappearance of one of the children who nobody has ever found."

"How many children do they have?"

"Three that I know of. Now there are only two."

The two trekked up the trail, then cut toward a different route which was difficult to walk in because of the deep snow. "That's the cabin right up there. It just gives me the creeps." She followed behind Chase as they walked up toward the house.

"The door is open a bit, and it looks like snow has gotten in."

"That's not good," Kady said, grabbing Chase's hand.

When they reached the house, Chase called in. "Is anyone home?" No answer. He gently pushed the door open, and there was a band of snow leading into the living room. The two stepped over it and stopped in shock. Four people sat in chairs with eyes that stared at nothing.

Chase check for a pulse on each of them as Kady trailed close behind him. "All four people are dead, but not from freezing to death." He pointed at their chests. "Bullet wounds in each of their hearts."

Kady covered her mouth and buried her head in Chase's chest. She finally peered up. "How do we know the killer is not still around?"

"We don't. Call the sheriff's department."

She looked at her phone. "Damn it, no cell service."

A rustling came from another room. Chase inched toward it. Kady held onto his coat and followed him. They both stopped when they saw a young man sitting down on the floor in tears. He had blood on his torn shirt, his hands were shaking holding a gun, and his eyes were bloodshot from tears.

He looked up at them. "I didn't want to kill them, but they gave me no choice." The young man lifted his gun and pointed it at Chase and Kady.

Chase took a deep breath. "Okay, put the gun down. We can work it out."

The man had a hysterical laugh. "Do you really think the law enforcement will look at it that way? They can't wait to stick a needle in me."

Chase took a step forward. "That's not true. The state has not executed a prisoner in decades, and they frown against doing something like that."

"How would you know anything about that? And Kady Boyd, she'd get off anyway, so what's the point?"

"I'm an attorney, and that's part of what I do."

The man lowered his gun a bit. "Would you

consider representing me? Of course not, because the Boyds won't allow it. Her father would rather have me executed in cold blood in one of his hunting expeditions in the mountains." He stared at Kady. "You know nothing about that, do you, Ms. Boyd. Yes, your father takes people out into the woods, executes them his way, and no one's the wiser because no one ever finds the body. That's what happened to my fiancée."

Chase spoke up. "You were going to marry her and she disappeared?"

"No, she didn't disappear. Darren Boyd took her, used her like he does all the other young women, and when they're not useful anymore, he does away with them."

Chase inched forward a bit while the guy was talking. "Then why would you kill her family?"

He wiped away tears. "They didn't do anything to protect her. They just let Darren Boyd do what he wanted to do."

Chase tried to move forward once more.

"Stop, or I'll put a bullet in your chest right now. I have one bullet left and I can't decide if I should kill you or Ms. Boyd. It would do her good to see the guy she loves die in front of her like her father did to me."

"You saw him murder your fiancée?"

"I didn't, but there's no doubt he did. When she called me the last time, she told me that she thought she was going to die because she wasn't good enough for Darren Boyd anymore. I never knew what that meant, but she's dead."

"How do you know she just didn't disappear or escape?"

"She would never leave me because we loved each

other." The man pointed his pistol at Chase. "I've decided you're the one who has to die."

"If I die, sure you may break Kady's heart, but she'll have seen everything, heard everything, and you'll get that needle you so badly detest. The best thing to do is just give me the pistol and see what we can work out."

He thought for a moment. "You're right because that's exactly what that bitch would do. She doesn't care about anyone but herself, and of course her father, who provides her with everything she wants."

Just like that he placed the gun under his throat and pulled the trigger, blood splattering everywhere. Kady screamed and buried her head into Chase's chest. Stunned, he wrapped his arms around her and tried to control her shaking.

Chapter 30

Sheriff Portal sat down with Kady and talked to her about what happened at the cabin. One of his deputies had taken Chase outside to interview him about what had happened. Several other county officers and the F.B.I. were looking for evidence at the scene.

After she was through giving the deputy her statement, the sheriff asked her, "to be clear, he was just sitting there on the floor weeping?"

"That's exactly what he was doing, Sheriff. I stood behind Chase, but he had his gun pointed at him and said he was going to pull the trigger so I'd feel the pain he did after my father killed his fiancée, who was the missing daughter of this family."

"Do you believe anything he said?"

Kady took a shuddering breath. "I have no idea what to think. I didn't believe my father was capable of that sort of thing, but now I question myself, especially after you arrested him for the kidnapping of the Native American girls."

"Is there anything else you can think of?"

Kady shook her head. "I can't think of anything

else. Is Chase okay?"

"As far as I know he is."

Once the deputy left, Kady hurried outside to Chase taking his hand. "Why did this have to happen? He didn't have to kill himself."

"I can't answer it. He was a crazy young man. Who knows what the truth is about what he said."

Kady was still shaking. Chase wrapped is arm around her, his voice gentle. "It's over now. Everything will be okay."

She peered up at Chase. "Will it? I've tried so hard to tell myself it'll get better, but it hasn't."

They both pivoted to see Karl racing toward her. She hugged him. "I've missed you so much."

The sheriff joined Chase after they left. "I wouldn't have expected anything like this at all. What do you think about his take on Darren Boyd?"

Chase searched the area before talking. "I've had my fill of shady, rich characters, including my family, so it wouldn't surprise me if what he had to say is true."

The sheriff nodded. "I wouldn't disagree there, especially after the incident with the Native American girls."

It was late Wednesday night when Chase drove out to the reservation to pick up Willa for the senior citizen's center event. As he drove through the reservation, he noticed the stares the people were giving him. He didn't know what to think. Chase found Willa's mother's rundown house, parked the Jeep, and walked up to knock on the door.

Willa's mother answered with her dress halfway down her shoulder. "Chase Connor, I'm sorry to tell you that Willa is not here. She asked me to give this letter to you when you showed up." She handed him an envelope, then shut the door in his face.

Chase climbed back into his Jeep, backed up, and drove back toward Mountain Ridge, not surprised with what had happened. Once he was off the reservation, he pulled into a spot off the road. He turned the Jeep off, then opened the envelope, finding a letter in it. He read it.

Chase, you knew this was going to happen that I wouldn't be able to handle a relationship with you as much as I want to. Eventually we both would realize it wouldn't work out. There is so much you don't know about me, just like there'd be things I would find out about you that I couldn't handle. More importantly, my little sister, Tanya, needs a new location, so that's where we're headed—to a new place where she can make a fresh start. I've never said this to a guy before, but I do love you. I wanted to tell you that the one night we were together, but I didn't have the courage, so it's much easier to tell you in a letter. I wish you a good life. I will love you and remember you as long as I live. Willa.

Chase put the letter back in the envelope, placed it into the cubby hole, and drove toward the senior citizen's center, arriving at five. He was introduced to several of the board members of the senior citizen's center, including Ophelia Shepherd. Her greeting was a bit chilly, probably because of the incident with her husband and the Native American girls.

It was five-thirty when the dinner started. It consisted of pork loin sandwiches and chips, something that Chase hadn't had in a long time. He sat with the board members at the head table, who extolled the wonderful features of the senior citizen's center.

At about six, Chase stepped up to the podium after being introduced by the board chairperson. He viewed the crowd, which included families and their children. He took a deep breath. "Thank you for inviting me to speak at your event. I'm honored to stand up before all of you who are involved with making sure our elders are taken care of. When I was asked to speak before you, I had no clue what they wanted me to talk about or even why they wanted me to tell my story."

He stopped to take a drink of his water. "It dawned on me just a half hour ago when I read a letter from a gal I care deeply about. She'd decided to leave the area so she could get a better start for her sister, something her parents should have done, but we all know that's not always possible. Her parents weren't there for her, but I see so many families out here tonight who care about their parents."

He sipped another drink of water. "Many of you know that I'm the son of a multi-billionaire in California but chose to escape to start a life of my own. Now I'm the owner of a bookstore and antique store, something I never thought I'd do but I actually enjoy it. I enjoy talking to the people who come in to tell me their stories. I enjoy helping them search for that book they've had a challenging time finding. Now I realize it's okay to do something my parents didn't want me to do. They're okay with it, although I didn't think that would ever be possible. So, I came to Montana to escape from my parents, but more importantly, I came to find out who I am. That's all my parents ever wanted, and I can see the happiness of all the elders in this room tonight because their children and grandchildren are living the lives they chose."

Chase took a deep breath before he continued. "I'm an attorney by trade, but I'm happy I decided to move into the bookstore and antique store business because it gives me time to think about who I'm becoming. While an attorney I didn't care for the person I was turning into. I worked for the rich and famous, many times knowing deep down they'd committed crimes, but my job was to get them off or find a way to reduce the sentence, which is what I did. It took a toll on me, my family, and the gals I dated."

He took another sip of his drink. "To sum it up, it's important to be who you are, not what your parents want you to be. To me, that's what constitutes a good life. I didn't think my parents would understand that, but they have, and I'm thankful for that."

After spending a couple of hours at the senior citizen's center, it was past ten when Chase entered the bookstore, locked it up, then crawled up the steps. He opened the door to the apartment, and noticed how dark it was. Willa had indeed decided to move on.

He sat on the couch, not sure whether to be sad or relieved. She was right, it would have never worked between the two of them, but it was all good because his last thoughts before he fell asleep were on Kady. He missed her.

Chapter 31

The week went by quickly at the bookstore. Harold Harper, the owner of the antique shop, invited him to join the family for a Saturday luncheon where they'd be able to talk about the antique store with his family there. Harold wanted his kids to ask any questions.

It was close to noon when Chase knocked on the door. A blond-haired gal, who was Chase's age, answered the door. "Can I help you?" She smiled.

"I'm Chase Connor. He invited me over to a luncheon this afternoon." They both turned when a couple of young boys came whipping down the hall.

"Slow down, you two," the young lady said.

"Yes, Auntie Ashley," they both said together.

Once they hurried away, Ashley turned to Chase. "As you can tell, my name is Ashley. Those two are not my sons but my sister's, and they have a lot of energy."

"I can tell that."

"Please join us. Dad is in the living room with other members of the family."

Chase and Ashley ambled into the living room where a group of grown-ups were talking. "Dad, Chase Connor to see you."

The man in the wheelchair pivoted toward the voice. "Good to see you once more, Mr. Connor."

"Please call me Chase."

"Chase, it is. Let me introduce you to my family. This is my oldest daughter, Kaci, and her husband, Stephen. They have four children. Laci, and her husband, Brett, have three children, and Maci and her husband, Ian Strong, have three children. Ashley, our youngest isn't married."

Laci interrupted. "Soon she will be after her boyfriend, Glen Allan, proposes to her."

Chase turned around to the voice casting his eye on Glen Allan, a man who stood a bit shorter than him, had black hair, with a mustache and a growth of beard.

"Well, Chase Connor, what brings you to Montana?"

Mr. Harper spoke up. "You know Chase?"

"Oh yes, the two of us graduated from Stanford University law as attorneys. He was tops in the class. Chase worked for a year with his father before deciding to hightail it away from California, and this is where he landed."

Ian Strong eyed him. "Who in their right mind would think about owning a bookstore or an antique shop when you could be a powerful attorney in California?"

"I had my reasons," Chase said.

He was saved by a woman's voice. "Time to eat, all." Mr. Harper patted Chase's leg. "My wife, Valeria, says it's time to eat so we should go."

They gathered around a large table in the dining room while the children sat at makeshift tables in another room within sight. Ashley helped her mother dish out the beef stew and biscuits. Once a blessing was said, they dipped into the beef stew.

"This is very good," Chase said. "Thank you for inviting me to join you for lunch."

Kaci eyed Chase. "You're interested in the antique store to go along with the bookstore next door?"

"I am, ma'am."

Valeria studied Chase. "Do you even know anything about antiques?"

"It's a pretty straightforward question," Chase said. "The simple answer to that is—an antique shop is a retail business specializing in the selling of antiques, but in my mind, it's much more than that." He sipped on his iced tea.

Chase peered around the kitchen table, then back to Harold. "Why are you interested in selling the business?"

"I hoped one of my daughters would be interested in taking the business over, but they're too busy with their own lives. I'm not in the condition I used to be in, so it's time to get out of the business. I know this is putting you on the spot, but what would your business model be?"

Chase slowly sipped on his drink thinking. "To start with, I'd combine both the antique store and bookstore together for more opportunities for customers. I would turn the upstairs in the antique store into a showroom for specific antiques and treasures that we bring in."

Mr. Harper nodded.

Laci jumped in. "What makes you think you can operate an antique store?"

Chase thought. "I'm not an expert by any means on antiques, but like the bookstore, I'll talk to experts in the field to make it a manageable, profitable business. I'll lean on you, Mr. Harper, when starting."

Harold laughed. "Once I sell the business, Valeria and I are taking that long-deserved vacation."

"Good for you," Chase said.

After lunch was over, everyone went back out into the living room. "Thank you for inviting me over today for lunch. It was wonderful," Chase said.

"You're welcome," Valeria said.

Harold covered his wife's hand. "It seems like the family is satisfied with what is happening, so we can proceed with completing the sale of the store. I'll set something up with the other attorney in town and let you know of the date and time."

Chase headed toward the door, but Ashley stopped him. "It was nice meeting you, Chase. Why don't you join us at the bar and grill tonight?"

"I'll think about it."

It was past eight when Chase strolled down to the bar and grill. He didn't know why, but he decided to join the Harpers. Chase ambled into the bar and grill, seeing it was another packed house.

He turned at a tap on his shoulder. "You decided to join us."

"Yes, I thought why not. You're Maci, correct?"

She smiled. "Yes, I am. We're over this way."

As they walked over to the corner where the others were, Chase asked her, "what did you do to your hair? It was blond."

"I added some tones, in this case they call it 'bouncy caramel blond.'"

"You look nice," Chase said.

"Thank you. Wait until you see my little sister."

Chase stopped when he saw Ashley talking to Glen Allan and others. She was beautiful.

Maci grinned. "She added brown, blond layers to her hair, and she darkened her eyebrows to help make her brown eyes stick out. She's a beauty."

"She is that." Chase turned to Maci. "I shouldn't have said that since she's with another guy."

Maci grinned. "Don't worry. I won't tell her if you don't."

The two joined the others. Ashley smiled at Chase. "I'm glad you decided to join us. Glen Allan went over to grab us some drinks, and he should be back anytime. What made you decide to join us?"

"I'm not sure. Guess it's good to get out of the bookstore to see others."

Glen Allan returned with a tray of drinks for the group. He grinned at Chase. "I bought you your favorite. Rum and coke, isn't it?"

"Thanks."

He took the drink and sipped it. Glen Allan eyed him. "That's not the Chase Connor I know. You would have downed that whole drink in one swig."

Chase sighed. "I've changed."

The group chatted for another hour before heading out on the dance floor. Chase watched them dance and listened to the music. Twenty minutes later Glen Allan and Ashley came over to join him. "Was it enjoyable?"

"It was," Glen Allan said. "But then everything about Ashley is enjoyable. I hit the jackpot with her."

Chase took another sip of his drink. "I'm happy for you."

Glen Allan grabbed his glass of wine. "I saw Kady Boyd the other day with her fiancé. Did you know they were getting married in June?"

"She said something about it."

"It's sad what happened with Dr. Boyd and his brother dealing with the missing girls."

Chase nodded. "At least the girls were found. What is it with you two?"

Glen Allan smiled. "We've been dating about two months now, and I believe I've found the gal of my dreams."

Chase turned to Ashley who peered into Chase's eyes. "I'm still debating on whether Glen Allan is the guy for me."

Chase turned to Glen Allan. "You wouldn't mind if I stole a dance with your girlfriend?"

"No, go ahead," he said, waving his hand. "I'm not too worried about you stealing her from me. We both know who you are."

Chase took Ashley's hand. "May I?"

She smiled. "You may."

The two strolled out onto the dance floor. She wrapped her hands around his neck, and he held his hands around her waist. "Thanks for agreeing to dance with me."

She peered into his eyes. "You're welcome. I hoped you'd asked me to dance." The two swayed to the music for a couple of slow songs.

"How did you meet Glen Allan?"

"I met him at one of the socials put on by Dr. Boyd. My dad always wanted us to participate in these business socials if it could help with the antique shop. I was usually the one designated because I was single. Maci has been to several also, but her husband, Ian, isn't too happy about her going to them. He's afraid she'll find someone better, which I hope she does."

"I noticed he's a bit older than her."

Ashley nodded. "He's twelve years older than she is, and the kids are not hers, but his first wife's. She's having a heckuva time with the boy. He wants nothing to do with her, and Ian doesn't help matters because he's not home enough."

Chase grinned. "Strong feelings about Ian."

"I'm sorry, but I just don't like the guy. Maci needs to find someone better." He heard her quietly say, "as long as it's not you."

Chase asked another question. "I noticed all your names on the Christmas stockings. Why doesn't your name have an 'I' at the end like your sisters?"

She stopped dancing, smiling at Chase. "You're the first person who's ever asked me that. I can't answer it because I have no clue."

"Kind of a stupid question, I imagine."

She peered up at him. "No, it isn't. I appreciate a guy who can think quickly on his feet. Glen Allan may be an attorney, but he isn't as quick-witted as you seem to be. Why is that?"

"Now, that's a question I can't answer."

She grinned. "Now we both have something to think about before the next time we meet."

Chase shook his head. "That probably won't happen since you're with Glen Allan."

"I wouldn't be too sure about that."

Once the fourth slow dance stopped, the two walked off the dance floor. "Thank you, I loved it," Ashley said. "I hope we can do this again someday." They joined the others at the table.

"Well, did you enjoy yourself?" Glen Allan asked.

Ashley shrugged. "It was okay. Our dance was much better."

Glen Allan grinned. "Chase, you always played second fiddle to me when it comes to gals."

"You're right. I should get going."

Ian frowned. "The night is still young. What's so important you would have to leave right now?"

Maci grasped his arm. "Ian, if the guy has to leave, let it be."

Ian eyed her. "Maybe you'd like to join him."

Maci frowned back at her husband. "Maybe I would, but my guess is Chase Connor wouldn't fool around with a married woman."

Glen Allan laughed. "He'd be the first Connor who didn't chase married women."

Chapter 32

Chase relaxed on his couch in his upstairs apartment watching a football game the next day. He wasn't necessarily watching the game as much as contemplating his life for the past four months.

It had been an adventure over that period of time with him purchasing a bookstore, on the verge of adding an antique store, and helping solve a kidnapping mystery that had been haunting the residents of Flathead County for the past year or so.

He chuckled to himself as he drank his iced tea. Chase had come to Montana to escape all the insanity that occurred in his life in California but found out it had followed him to the fourth largest state in the union behind California, Alaska, and Texas.

He had met a group of people who made him feel like he was part of a family, something that had never occurred in California. He and his only sister, Samantha, were close, but the others were a bit more distant.

Then there were the women in Montana. Sophia was a beautiful model, then Meredith was right where she should be, on her way to becoming a doctor. He and Willa would have never worked out, since she would always have trust issues from growing up in her family. Then there was Kady.

"Are you daydreaming, Chase?"

Chase snapped out of his thought process and saw Kady grinning at him. "Are you dreaming about me once more?"

"Actually, I was. Along with Sophia, Meredith, and Willa."

Kady laughed and dropped down on the couch next to him. "You really need to lock your bookstore, especially after you had a book stolen. Here you are watching a football game. You know I love football."

"I do. What brings you up here?"

She reached over to take his hand. "I wanted to have a deep conversation with you to see where we're at together, or if we could be together. Karl has a wonderful job opportunity out east, and he's seriously considering the job."

"That's wonderful news for the two of you. I'm happy for you."

She smiled. "Thanks. Before I move out east with him, I need to know if there is any chance for the two of us. I do love you, but I'm not sure where you stand. If you love me, I'll stay right here with you. If you don't, then I'm heading east right after Christmas."

Chase sighed. "Kady, I loved you once also, but that seems like a long time ago. The few times we've been together since I've been in Montana have brought back some of those wonderful memories, but the two of us will never be. You deserve so much more, and you have it with Karl. Please go east with him, forget about me, and have the life you want."

She wiped a tear from her cheek. "I feel so much better that I can let my past with you go. Know that I enjoyed every moment we had together, but you're right. The past is over and it's time for both of us to move forward with our lives." She reached over, framed his face, and gently kissed him on the lips. "This is the last time we'll see each other. Enjoy your life with someone you love. Don't settle for anyone less because you deserve a wonderful life also."

Chase walked down the stairs with Kady. The two hugged one more time before she headed over to the car where Karl was waiting for her. Chase waved at him and Karl returned it. Once the two drove away, Chase turned back to close the door. He no sooner closed the door when there was a knock. He spun around and opened the door.

There stood Sheriff Portal.

"Sheriff, what can I do for you?"

He handed him a package.

"What is this?"

"I was hoping you could help me figure out why someone would mail this to me without a note or anything."

"What is it?"

The sheriff pulled a book out of the envelope and handed it to Chase. Chase read the title, *Mountain Ridge Mysteries*. The two stared blankly at each other. "It's a book, but what does this mean?"

"You got me. That's why I stopped by to see if you knew what it was all about. You're the book expert now."

Chase laughed. "Let's get started figuring it out."

THE END

Other books by this author
Bouncing Back
The Battle Off the Court
Freedom Flight
Fight for Survival
Road to Hell
A New Life Begins
Relentless
Missing
Targeted

Author Bio: My wife, Susan and I have two sons, Justin (Kayla) and Jeremy and a grandson, Aiden. Born and raised in South Dakota. I enjoy spending time with family, traveling and putt-putt. I recently retired as managing editor of a small town Iowa newspaper. I am a former Marine Corps veteran, getting my start in the publishing business in 1981 working for several years on base newspapers. I spent time running my own freelance business. I love writing. I enjoy reading anything and everything. I also love the history of our country and enjoy reading western books, mysteries, and adventure novels, and watching mystery, adventure, and western movies.

224